KILL AND KILL AGAIN

A JULIAN QUIST MYSTERY NOVEL

ALSO BY HUGH PENTECOST

Pierre Chambrun Mystery Novels:

Nightmare Time
Remember to Kill Me
Murder in High Places
With Intent to Kill
Murder in Luxury
Beware Young Lovers
Random Killer
Death after Breakfast
The Fourteen Dilemma
Time of Terror
Bargain with Death
Walking Dead Man
Birthday, Deathday
The Deadly Joke
Girl Watcher's Funeral

Julian Quist Mystery Novels:

The Party Killer
Substitute Victim
Murder Out of Wedlock
Past, Present, and Murder
Sow Death, Reap Death
Death Mask
The Homicidal Horse
Deadly Trap
The Steel Palace
Die after Dark

Uncle George Mystery Novels:

Death by Fire
Murder Sweet and Sour
The Price of Silence
The Copycat Killers

HUGH PENTECOST

DODD, MEAD & COMPANY
NEW YORK

Published by Dodd, Mead & Company, Inc.
71 Fifth Avenue
New York, New York 10003
Distributed in Canada by
McClelland and Stewart Limited, Toronto
Manufactured in the United States of America

First Edition

1 2 3 4 5 6 7 8 9 10

Library of Congress Cataloging-in-Publication Data

Pentecost, Hugh, 1903–
Kill and kill again.

I. Title.
PS3531.H442K5 1987 813′.52 87-452
ISBN 0-396-08898-8

KILL AND KILL AGAIN

A JULIAN QUIST MYSTERY NOVEL

PART 1

Chapter One

The disappearance of Martha Best in the small city of Bridgetown, miles up the west shore of the Hudson River from New York, would have been pretty much a local story except for one fact: Martha's brother was Wally Best, the popular and highly successful country singer and recording artist. Suddenly the story was everywhere, with probably millions of fans rooting for "Wally's sister." Television news shows caught Wally Best's usually smiling face twisted by anxiety and grief as the days wore on. One has to wonder how many viewers would have recognized Martha from the photographs shown even if they'd come face to face with her on the street. Wally Best was the star of the show, but Martha, police came to believe, was its tragic victim. The morning of the ninth day there hadn't been a trace of her. She was to be found later that morning in a place where she hadn't been on the morning of the first day.

Apart from her connection to Wally Best, Martha's disappearance followed a fairly routine pattern. Secretary for a prominent Bridgetown businessman, Martha left her office about five-thirty on a Wednesday evening in February. The doorman in her office building remembered cautioning her to "bundle up" as she left for the day. No one gave her a second thought until the next day, when she failed to turn up for work. She lived alone in an apartment on the east side of Bridgetown, overlooking the now-ice-clogged river. There was no one to take notice of the fact that she didn't come home Wednesday night.

Martha's car had been ticketed and towed away by police before midnight on that Wednesday. Special parking regulations had been imposed because the threat of a blizzard had made the place where she'd parked her canary yellow Mercedes-Benz, normally legal, illegal. That place was about three blocks away from the office building where she worked. Some oddities about that developed as hours and days wore on without any word from the missing woman. Martha always parked her car in a reserved space in back of the building where she worked. It had been parked there that Wednesday. The lot attendant remembered suggesting that she bring a snow shovel with her when she came to work the next day. She'd driven less than three blocks, pulled over to the curb, and left her Mercedes there with the keys still in the ignition. That must have been at about a quarter of six. The special parking regulations hadn't gone into effect until ten o'clock, and the yellow Mercedes hadn't been towed away until about eleven. This suggested that Martha had parked and left her car for what was expected to be only a few moments. There was a Mom-and-Pop grocery store right where she'd parked, but no one remembered a young lady stopping in, say for a pound of coffee or a pound of butter. The owners didn't remember ever seeing the woman in the photograph police showed them later. The yellow Mercedes had been where Martha had left it when the Guardinos, the store owners, closed up shop at eight o'clock. The yellow Mercedes wasn't a car you overlooked. It seemed a pretty fancy car for a girl who worked in an office until some enterprising reporter discovered that it had been a gift from her famous brother, Wally Best.

Martha had been a young woman with reddish-blond hair, all the proper curves, and an inviting smile. She hadn't used these assets in a provocative fashion, but certainly some kind of sexual maniac wouldn't have passed her by. Sexual assault was the best guess police could make in those first days. Someone could be holding her prisoner somewhere, or her dead body had been hidden away somewhere no one had yet explored.

When Martha Best didn't turn up on time for work on Thursday morning, her boss, Mark Foreman, president of Manchester Arms, Bridgetown's major business, wasn't too concerned. The storm of the night before had indeed reached blizzard proportions. Transportation, both public and private, was near impossible. But as eleven o'clock approached, Mark Foreman put in a call to Martha Best's apartment. No answer. Shortly after that the police called Foreman's office. They had been trying to reach Martha to tell her where her car was. Getting no answer at her apartment, they'd found her business address and number in the glove compartment of the Mercedes.

"That was when we started to worry," Foreman told reporters. "Whatever happened to her must have taken place in the early evening hours of Wednesday."

Wally Best, idol of pop-music fans around the world, was on a concert tour in California when word got to him that his sister was missing. He arrived in Bridgetown during the early hours of Friday morning, some thirty hours after Martha had parked her Mercedes outside the Guardinos' grocery store. He promptly posted a $25,000 reward to anyone who could provide information that would lead to Martha's safe return. Wally wasn't prepared to face the really grim possibilities in the situation.

Day after day went by, however, and even the most classic optimist couldn't hold out much hope for Martha. The police didn't have the ghost of a clue. Martha hadn't contacted any friends, at least no one who came forward. On that stormy Wednesday evening, people had been in too great a hurry to get home and batten down the hatches to notice a passerby on the street. The Mercedes had been carefully examined for fingerprints, inside and out. There were none, not even Martha's. But that wasn't too strange. On that bitterly cold night people would have been wearing gloves.

Wally Best, impatient for results, hired a private detective from New York City named George Klugman. After three days on the case, Klugman had come up with nothing.

"I guess we have to start back at square one," Klugman told Wally. "That's the car, the last place she was seen alive, driving out of her office parking lot by the attendant there."

So it was that on that ninth day Klugman came up with the terrible truth about what had happened to Martha. He found her, locked in the trunk of the yellow Mercedes, frozen stiff in death. The city's medical examiner couldn't perform an autopsy to determine the cause of death until the body thawed out, but it seemed probable that Martha had been sexually assaulted, probably strangled in the process.

The first question reporters asked was how the police could have missed finding the body in the car's trunk when they first took the Mercedes in. The answer, eventually supplied by Captain Walter Seaton, head of Bridgetown's homicide police, added to the mystery.

"There was no reason to search the trunk of the car when it was first towed in," Seaton said. "Miss Best's keys were in the ignition, her registration and other identification in the glove compartment. There was no reason to search the trunk then. The car had been taken in for violating an emergency parking regulation. It really wasn't a crime. The only 'penalty' Miss Best would have incurred was the inconvenience of getting her car back from the police parking lot. It wasn't until Thursday afternoon that it was reported to us that something may have happened to Miss Best."

"Something?" a reporter asked.

"She was missing, unaccounted for," Seaton said. "Officers went back to the car to search for fingerprints. In the process they opened the trunk. So we know that late Thursday afternoon the girl's body wasn't where it was found today."

"For God's sake, Captain," the reporter said, "that means the body was put in the trunk of the car, right there in the police parking lot, sometime after Thursday evening!"

Seaton nodded. "That's the way it appears to be."

"No guards, no watchmen, where police are holding hundreds of thousands of dollars' worth of other people's property?"

"There's a watchman," Seaton said, "and an army of officers in police headquarters, right at the rear of the lot."

"Yet someone could carry a body into the lot and store it in the trunk of a car?"

"Until we have another explanation, that's the way it is," Seaton said.

Now it was a national story in spades. Pictures of Martha Best appeared on television, films, and in every newspaper in the country—printed alongside pictures of her famous brother, Wally. No one who wasn't blind or stone-deaf could have escaped it. Radio blared out the story every fifteen minutes around the clock. Finally Wally Best posted a $100,000 reward for information leading to the capture and conviction of his sister's murderer. Then days, weeks, and actually months went by without any real response to Wally Best's reward offer. Bridgetown police had covered every single lead several times over and had still come up empty. New terror stories and juicy scandal items took over the public interest. Whatever had happened to Martha Best faded somewhere into a murky past.

It was August.

The offices of the public relations firm of Julian Quist Associates are located halfway up a steel-and-glass finger pointing to the sky, just north of Grand Central Terminal in New York City. Julian Quist, tall, blond, with a profile that might have been carved on an ancient Greek coin, is probably more familiar to the people of the press, television, and radio than some of his famous clients. He has the talent to turn a pumpkin into a princess, and it has happened too often for anyone to think of it as accidental.

On a hot August morning, Quist's study of some documents and photographs was interrupted by his private secretary, Connie Parmalee. "A surprise visitor," Connie told her boss. "Wally Best."

Quist put down his papers. "Wally! I didn't expect—"

"He doesn't have an appointment," Connie said. She was tall and thin, with a good figure, red hair, and the proper legs for a miniskirt if they were in fashion at the time. "But I thought you'd want to see him."

"Of course," Quist said.

Ten years before, Wally Best had been a green kid out of a small Hudson River city, Bridgetown, with a talent for country music. Quist and his partners had helped turn him into an international star.

Tragedy had aged the young singer. He came into Quist's office and stood just inside the door, not speaking.

Quist walked over and put his hand on Wally's shoulder. "I don't know what to say to you, man," he said. "I wrote you a note when the story broke offering to help if I could, but I suppose it got lost in a mountain of mail from fans and friends."

"No," Wally said. "But I didn't need help—then."

Quist didn't miss the hesitation. "But now?"

"Can we talk?"

"Of course. Come in, sit down. Coffee?"

Wally just shrugged and headed for the chair by Quist's desk.

Quist detoured by way of the Mr. Coffee machine on a side table and brought two china mugs of coffee over to the desk. "It must be ghastly knowing that there's some kind of sex maniac floating around Bridgetown and not having any kind of lead to him."

A nerve twitched at the corner of Wally's mouth. "I don't believe that any longer, Julian," he said. "That's why I'm here." He didn't go on.

"It's your ball game, Wally," Quist said. "Play it."

Wally took a sip of his coffee and let his breath out in a long sigh. "About two weeks before Martha disappeared, I paid her a visit in Bridgetown. When I'm in this area I always go there, not only to see Martha, but because I grew up there."

"But you have no other family left there, as I remember."

"No. All gone—including Martha, now."

Quist waited. Some kind of story was coming.

"About two weeks before Martha disappeared I went there to see her. She—she was in very high spirits. 'I may be just about to blow you off the front pages, brother dear,' she told me."

"She found she could sing?"

Wally shook his head. "Nothing to do with music at all," he said. "Martha worked for a man named Mark Foreman, who's president of Manchester Arms. Manchester Arms *is* Bridgetown. They manufacture all kinds of weaponry—handguns, rifles, automatic weapons, grenades, bombs. The tools of war—" and Wally's mouth tightened. "War and terror."

"It gets mentioned outside of Bridgetown," Quist said.

"Hundreds of jobs in the town," Wally said. "An airport that can handle transcontinental jets, docks on the river that can handle overseas shipping. Manchester Arms is a billion-dollar world."

"What does this have to do with Martha making headlines?" Quist asked.

"Details I didn't get to know, but the overall picture is of trading with the enemy, selling to terrorists like that creep in Libya, to the Central American communists; bribes paid to big-shot politicians in Washington. A foot in the door of local and state politics. Corruption in spades! Martha had facts and figures, she told me. A couple more manholes to open up, and she was ready to blow the guilty persons at Manchester Arms sky-high. Tomorrow or the next day—"

"A dangerous game," Quist said.

"Murder means no tomorrow," Wally said. "There was no tomorrow for Martha. It was made to look like a rape, a sexual orgy of some sort. I've come to believe it was Manchester Arms, the city of Bridgetown, making sure it survived."

"Why the elaborate hiding of her body, putting it back in her car? Wouldn't it have been simpler to dump her body in the river?"

"She had to be found with evidence to prove that a sexual maniac was responsible, not a cold-blooded business empire that would kill and kill again if it was necessary. It hasn't ever been suggested in Bridgetown that it was anything but a sexual horror. Those bastards walking around saying how sorry they are, how tragic it was!"

"Martha left nothing behind that would show what she was working on?" Quist asked.

"Nothing in her office, nothing in her apartment," Wally said. "Everything checked out, clean as a whistle. I think that's why we were kept from finding her for days. They were making sure there wasn't a trace of what she'd been up to. When they were sure there was nothing anywhere that could trap them, they let us find her, with evidence that it had been a sex crime."

"So this is all guesswork?"

"I've had a private detective on the job from the very beginning. Nothing!"

"No response to your offer of a huge reward?"

"A few crackpots. Nothing real."

"So—you suggested at the start of this conversation that there might be some way I could help you. I'm not a detective, Wally."

"Fasten your seat belt, Julian," Wally said.

Quist gave his friend a wry smile. "It's fastened, chum."

"This is an election year," Wally said. "I propose to run for the office of mayor of Bridgetown."

Quist stared at him, unblinking. "That's a little too fast for me, Wally."

"If I were elected mayor, I'd have access to every corrupt act, every treacherous deal. I could hang these monsters for what they did to Martha in the town square for the whole damn world to see."

"Or die in the attempt," Quist said, not smiling.

"It would be worth the risk," Wally said.

"So where does Julian Quist Associates fit into the picture?" Quist asked.

"Handle my campaign. Get me elected," Wally said.

Quist sat silent for a moment. He had helped promote more than one political candidate over the years: a United States senator, at least two congressmen, the mayor of a big midwestern city. But those men had all had qualifications for their jobs—political histories that were assets, plus the support of major party machines. Wally Best had none of those things going for him. Quist told him so.

"It's true I don't have a political party behind me," Wally said. "Both major parties in Bridgetown are supported by Manchester Arms. I might not even get on the ballot. It might have to be a write-in vote. But with your skills—"

"Hold on just one minute," Quist said. "What do I have to sell?"

Wally's smile was bitter. "I'm a local kid who made good. I made Bridgetown famous with my gold record, 'The Rat Pack Lover.' I've been through a tragedy in their town. I deserve something from them. There are thousands of voters who would like me, want to do something for me."

"And you're out to show up corruption?"

"Not that!" Wally said sharply. "Let the local bad boys hear that and I will join Martha—wherever she is! You sell sentiment for a nice guy, and I play 'nice guy' all over the map until I'm in."

"These people you're out to get in Bridgetown," Quist said. "Are they too stupid to realize why you might be running for office?"

"No, I don't think so, but just running for office isn't enough. I'd have to get elected to be any kind of threat to them. I'm sure, in the early stages, they'll be certain I don't stand a chance. They have controlled elections for the last twenty-five years. I can raise some pretty impressive cash, thanks to my success as a performer, but nothing to match what they can lay hands on. They won't see me as any kind of threat to them until I wind up in the mayor's office, appoint my friends to key positions, open up their Pandora's box."

"Is there really the remotest chance that can happen, Wally?"

"Nice guy," Wally said, "famous entertainer who's made millions happy, out for something that would honor his murdered sister. If we can get everyone in Bridgetown to the polls, there are enough sentimentalists to win over the votes Manchester Arms can buy. I've got enough money to finance television, radio, and any other kind of media exposure you suggest. I can act any role you decide I should play. You dream it up, and we may come in on a tidal wave the Manchester boys won't realize is coming until it's too late." Wally leaned forward in his chair. "Will you take it on, Julian? Will you help me bury those killers in their own garbage?"

Quist hesitated. "Let me put it to my brain trust," he said.

Quist's "brain trust" consisted of four people. First there was Lydia Morton, a lovely red-haired lady who was the top researcher and writer for Quist Associates and who shared an apartment with Quist on Beekman Place. Asked why he and Lydia didn't marry, Quist had a pat answer: "We started living in sin, and it has been so perfect we can't risk changing a single detail of it."

There was Dan Garvey, dark, intense, who had been an all-star running back in the National Football League. He handled all the sports promotions for Quist, and he was a very good man to have on one's side if the going got rough.

There was Bobby Hilliard, who looked like a young Jimmy Stewart—the Jimmy Stewart of fifty years ago. He was a genius at raising money for charity, and a perfect agent for handling the causes of rich old ladies.

Finally, there was Connie Parmalee, Quist's secretary, who could anticipate what he wanted before he'd thought of it himself.

Wally Best had hardly closed his mouth after telling his story to the brain trust when Dan Garvey spoke up.

"My answer is absolutely no!" he said. "We'd be playing with a loaded gun. These characters have killed, and they'll kill again."

Lydia Morton was looking at Wally with a lazy smile. "I think I could write a script for Wally selling him to Alaskan Indians. It would be fun to see if it can be done."

Bobby Hilliard produced his young Jimmy Stewart smile. "It would be easy to sell Wally to my kind of customers, old ladies dying to involve themselves in something romantic—a young man trying to honor his sister by heading up their town for a few years."

Quist glanced at Connie Parmalee.

"If I were sure you were going to lose, Julian, I might say yes. But you don't play to lose, do you?"

Quist nodded. "That makes it two for and two against," he said. "That leaves it up to me, doesn't it?" He was silent for a moment, and then he turned to Wally Best. "Let's make the preliminary moves, Wally. A nationwide announcement, then cover Bridgetown and see how they react there. We can always back off if it looks hopeless."

"Thanks, Julian," Wally said. "Thank you very much."

Chapter Two

Undertaking Wally Best's campaign for mayor of Bridgetown was a unique experience for Quist. It was the first time in his career that his client didn't want what he was after for the reasons he gave. Wally wasn't seeking political office to honor his late sister. He wasn't trying to fulfill a dream of hers, that he would someday be the head man in their home town. Wally was out to trap the men who had decided his sister must be eliminated, to trap the man who had actually killed her, and to trap the men who were covering up the crime. Dan Garvey put it neatly. "You'll have to talk sentimental garbage out of one corner of your mouth and keep the other corner zipped up tight," he told Quist. It would have been simpler, Quist told himself, to open up with both barrels, tell the truth about Wally's motives, and demand justice for his dead sister. Independent voters would buy that, but thousands of people caught in the world of Manchester Arms would have used all the influence they had to make sure Wally didn't make it. So they would have to present a nice, sentimental guy who could sing his way into heaven, not an angry man looking for justice and revenge.

"You're just not thinking clearly, Julian," Dan Garvey said, playing the prophet of doom from the very beginning. "The characters Wally is after in Bridgetown aren't going to be fooled for a minute. You've got roughly three months to election day. They'll play it cool until they see there's a chance Wally might win. Then they'll cave the roof in on him, and you, and anyone else involved with him. These characters play for keeps, Julian. If Wally's motives were what he pretends they are, I'd think you were an idiot for wasting time with this, unless you thought it would promote his singing career. As it is, I think you're just putting your neck on the chopping block, and the wrong guys have the axe!"

Quist listened and was silent for a while. Then he let it all out. "I don't think I'm doing this just for Wally, Dan. Back when we first knew him and were trying to get his music career going, Martha was very much in the picture. She was a nice, decent girl trying to help her brother get launched. She was someone I knew and liked. Now I find there's a corner of the world where life is a cheap commodity, where vicious violence is everyday, accepted by a whole group. It may sound absurd to you, Dan, but I don't want to live in a world where people get away with that kind of thing. I'm going to help Wally to do what he wants because I think it's a way to mow those characters down. I'm going to be with him, shoulder to shoulder, all the way, because I want what he wants—justice for Martha."

"So you want to be a hero!"

"I want to sleep at night," Quist said.

The brutal murder of Martha Best came back into the public eye a few days later when press, radio, and television announced Wally Best's intention to run for mayor of Bridgetown. The announcement was carefully and expertly staged by Julian Quist Associates. There was a simple press release to every newspaper, radio station, and television station in the country. There was a feature article, written by Lydia Morton, describing Wally's "boyhood dream" to become the head man in his home town; now, following his sister's tragic death, he wanted to make that dream come true as a gesture that would honor her. There was a television interview with Wally, handled by Larry Connors, a top network commentator, in which Wally talked about his "dream." It was dramatic by virtue of its planned lack of drama. He was going to run for mayor of Bridgetown to honor his beloved sister. Hundreds of thousands of viewers had never heard of Bridgetown, but they all knew Wally, the Rat Pack Lover, and they wished him well, wished they could vote for him. "Best is best for Bridgetown" was the slogan coined by Quist.

It was underway.

Going to Bridgetown was, for Quist, like going to a foreign country. He knew no one there except Wally, who was to act as his guide, introduce him to some of the key residents. In the days when Quist had worked starting Wally's musical career, the city of Bridgetown hadn't been important. Now, as he drove across the bridge that took them from the east side of the Hudson to the west shore, Wally pointed out the towering brick chimneys that marked the location of the Manchester Arms factories.

"I used to be proud of those," Wally said. "They were welcoming beacons when I came home. Now they represent 'the scene of the crime.' "

The size of the population determines whether a place is a village, a town, or a city. Twenty-five thousand residents made Bridgetown a city, about the size of Kingston, a little farther up the river.

"Tell me about the man we're going to see first," Quist said to Wally as they waited for a traffic light to change.

"Jerry Collins?" Wally asked. "I'm afraid it's going to be a waste of time." With Quist at his side, the campaign started, Wally seemed to have lost some of his early enthusiasm.

Maybe Dan Garvey's pessimism was partly responsible; maybe just getting closer to reality made his chances of success seem dimmer.

"Your hometown newspaper has to pay attention to you," Quist said.

"Oh, Jerry Collins will print press releases, but he won't plug for me. He's been in the Republican corner in Bridgetown ever since I was old enough to read."

"Bridgetown is Republican controlled?"

"Bridgetown is controlled by Manchester Arms," Wally said. "Manchester Arms is big money, which is usually Republican, isn't it? The reason there's any chance at all for me is that Fred Marple, who has been mayor for at least five terms, can't run again. Too old and sick. So at least we're going to be facing a new man—but hand-picked by Manchester Arms. The *Bridgetown Journal* and Jerry Collins will support that new man. That's as traditional as Christmas!"

"Collins is a Bridgetown native?"

"Third generation," Wally said. "His grandfather founded the *Journal*, his father ran it for almost fifty years, Jerry's been at the controls for the last ten or so. Manchester Arms has helped the *Journal* over some rough spots in the last century. They owe."

"So much for freedom of the press," Quist said.

"You don't have to be a cynic to say that's the way it is in most places," Wally said. "Big-business advertising keeps the press going everywhere, which means big business can control where the news media stand on local issues." Wally's tone was angry. "That's why I'll have to spend a half-million bucks to have any chance at all to win an election here."

The city of Bridgetown is built on a large area of sloping ground starting at the river's edge and rising upward. The result is that there is scarcely a piece of level ground that hasn't been engineered by men. Quist was to remark later, with some bitterness, that there was "nothing on the level in Bridgetown." It was a clean-looking town, he thought that first morning, sidewalks watered down and swept, no litter in the streets, shrubs and flowers outside some buildings, obviously carefully cared for. If there was poverty or neglect anywhere, Quist didn't see it on the way to the office of the *Bridgetown Journal* at the top of the town.

"I'm impressed," Quist told Wally. "It's not like the usual factory town."

"It's not," Wally said. "Manchester Arms has to make sure it doesn't look like the plucked chicken it really is."

The *Bridgetown Journal* was located at what had once been a farm at the top of the rise. The editorial and business offices were in what had once been the farmhouse. The presses and other mechanical features were in a rebuilt barn next to the house. The view down over the rooftops to the river was spectacular.

"What a place to work!" Quist said.

"If that work doesn't sour your stomach," Wally said.

Quist had discovered in the last few days that to go anywhere publicly with Wally Best was to become the center of an almost hysterical attention. Now, as they walked into the *Journal* office, fingers froze over typewriter keyboards, raised eyes were wide and bright, and there was a humming sound from a dozen voices all murmuring at once. "Wally Best!"

A door at the far end of the outer office opened before Quist and Wally had advanced three steps, and a man emerged. He was, Quist guessed, in his mid-forties with prematurely white hair, very black eyebrows shading bright blue eyes, smiling a smile that had to be professional.

"Wally!" the man said, approaching with his hand held out. "We've been wondering when you'd get to where the game has to be played." He turned his bright eyes on Quist. "You must be Julian Quist. I'm Jerry Collins." His handshake was firm, almost too firm. "Come into my office."

"If it's not a convenient time—" Quist said.

Collins reached out and put his hand on Wally's shoulder. "There's never an inconvenient time to talk to a man who's running for mayor—and for a celebrity like yourself, Mr. Quist. Come in! Come on in!"

A young woman rose from behind her typewriter and blocked Wally's path. "Can I have your autograph, Wally?"

Collins laughed. "You're going to need fillers for your ball-point pen, Wally. They're going to be lining up here in Bridgetown. Home-town hero! Take him on the way out, girls."

"The problem is going to be having people line up at the polls," Quist said.

"Ah, yes. Come in, gentleman. Coffee? There's a pot over there by the window."

Another young woman, obviously Collins's secretary, was staring at Wally.

"Hi, Cindy," Wally said.

"Oh, hi, Wally."

"Old high school friends," Wally said. "This is Julian Quist, Cindy."

"Cindy—?"

"Just Cindy," she said.

"I don't know you well enough to be on a first-name basis with you, Miss—?"

"I'm surprised you're not familiar with the way it is today," Collins interrupted. "Today everybody is just Cindy, or Nancy, or Sally. Last names are old hat!" He gestured to chairs. "You're going to complain that I haven't used the releases you've sent out, Quist, in the *Journal.*"

"I'm curious," Quist said. "It's Wally's home town. It is, as you said, the place where the game is going to be played."

Collins's smile looked pasted on, not real at all. "I like to get my information first hand, not on a mimeographed release," he said.

"So here we are," Wally said. "What do you need to know that you don't already know?"

The smile was totally erased now. "You've announced that you're running for mayor," Collins said.

"True."

"Are you really running for mayor, Wally, or is it just a promotional gag for your concerts and records?"

"I'm really running for mayor," Wally said.

"Not backed by either major party?"

"But by thousands of fans who love what he does," Quist said.

Collins's smile returned. "I haven't always loved you, Wally," he said. "Not when my kids played that 'Rat Pack Lover' record of yours over and over and over again!"

"But would you vote for him?" Quist asked.

Collins looked straight at Wally. "Why should I?"

"To begin with, Fred Marple isn't going to run again. You're not bound by any loyalty to him this time around," Wally said. "Whoever you vote for, it will be for a new mayor."

"But why you, Wally? The other candidates have political records. They've been in city management most of their adult lives. You've been titillating bobbysoxers."

" 'Bobbysoxers' is just about as out of date as last names," Quist said.

Collins ignored the remark. "You don't have a Chinaman's chance, and you must know it, Wally."

"I'm not so sure," Quist said, answering for Wally. "The murder of Wally's sister has the whole country wishing him well. He's running for mayor because it was a dream he and Martha had when they were kids. He wants it to come true now—for Martha. A great many people will buy that. After all, the city government will still be in its place. Manchester Arms will still be in its heaven and all will be right with the world."

"So go to Manchester Arms and get them to back you," Collins said. "Do that, and the *Journal* will back you."

"And if Mark Foreman and his boys say no?" Wally asked.

"The *Journal* has supported the Republican candidates for office since my grandfather's day, Wally—almost a century. He felt, and my father felt, and I feel that it is better for the town if we support the candidate who has the backing of the town's most important business. Without Manchester Arms, we'd revert to being a cow pasture. I'm sure there have been some good men who've run against Fred Marple and others who preceded him. But I think it has been healthy for the town to have Manchester's candidate in charge."

"And there's the advertising," Quist said. "Must pay a good part of your operating costs."

"All right," Collins said. "But it can be a good thing for the community even if it does turn a profit for the *Journal.* This time Greg Martin will head the Republican ticket, and we'll have to go along with him."

"But will you cover the campaign?" Quist asked. "You won't ignore the fact that Wally will be running as an independent?"

The professional smile reappeared. "I don't think you'll let me, will you, Quist? Every other paper in the state and the country, every radio and television station, will be carrying your handouts on Wally. I can't pretend he doesn't exist. I couldn't if I wanted to, and I don't want to. Personally I could go for you, boy, but politically I don't think you've got what the job calls for."

"Are the people of Bridgetown satisfied with an unresolved murder, with a city police force and management that can't find an answer?" Quist asked.

"Let me assure you of one thing, Quist," Collins said. "The city government wants that crime solved just as badly as Wally wants it solved. Martha was Mark Foreman's secretary at Manchester. He liked her and admired her. He has his own security people working night and day for an answer."

"It's seven months now," Wally said.

"So, a lunatic strikes and evaporates. The police haven't found a clue, Manchester's security people haven't found a clue, my reporters have come up empty, Wally's private detective found nothing."

"He found Martha's body," Wally said.

"At least we can thank God for that," Collins said. "You haven't had to spend all this time wondering."

"Well, at least we know where you stand," Quist said. "Local people are going to have to listen to radio and watch television if they're interested in Wally's campaign."

"Oh, we'll cover it," Collins said. "But we'll be supporting Greg Martin." As Quist rose to go, Collins raised his hand.

"This is Jerry Collins speaking, not the editor of the *Journal.* You know Maggie Nolan, Wally?"

Wally nodded. He explained to Quist. "Old lady, character here in Bridgetown. Runs a shelter for stray animals."

"And a shelter for pregnant teenagers," Collins said. "And all her life she's been an opponent of the two-party system and a staunch supporter of independents. She's as rich as God, and she might be persuaded to go all out for Wally. She could be a great organizer for you in this town, boy."

"Get all the crackpots on my side," Wally said.

"That's what you need," Collins said. "All the sentimental crackpots in town. Try your case out on Maggie. She just might go for it."

Quist got a rundown on Maggie Nolan from Wally on their way to the old lady's house at the top of the town.

"Must be damn near eighty now," Wally said.

"Miss or Mrs. Nolan?" Quist asked.

"As far as I know she never married. Her father was Hubert Nolan, made a fortune in drugs." Wally chuckled. "Not today's kind of drugs. Drugstore drugs! I don't know what brought Maggie to Bridgetown. I was too young to care when she came. She bought this farm at the top of town, turned it into a mansion. She busied herself with cleaning up Bridgetown—the streets, the sidewalks, the houses in the poorer section. She didn't want anything in return, so people said she was crazy, but they were grateful to her. She set up this haven for stray dogs, and when I was five or six, I used to hang around there, even brought her a couple that parked on my family's doorstep."

"So you're friends before we start," Quist said.

"I hope so. It's been almost ten years since I've seen her. She came to the one concert I had here, back at the start. But that's that."

"Mansion" wasn't an overstatement for the gracious house at the top of the hill. Not pretentious but gracious, Quist thought, with beautifully cared-for lawns and gardens surrounding it. They drove up to the parking area just outside the front door and stopped. As Quist turned off his motor, he was aware of music from a radio, television set, or record player.

"My God, that's me!" Wally said. " 'Rat Pack Lover'!"

Quist remembered the song. It had been Wally's first big hit.

I'm a Rat Pack bad guy,
But I'm the one who loves you.
I'm a Rat Pack hoodlum
But I'm the guy who loves you.
I write dirty words on the schoolhouse wall,
People don't think I stand very tall.
Because of the way I am
The cops make me stay under cover,
But never forget, I'm your Rat Pack Lover.

Long ago, Wally had explained to Quist that there had been a "rat pack" here in Bridgetown and that he'd been one of the tough guys in the pack. He'd written the song himself, and it had helped to launch his career. Quist didn't understand to this day what made a song grow popular. Maybe it was Wally's personality that had started him on the way to fame and fortune. But the "Rat Pack" song had been the beginning.

The front door to the mansion opened, and a tall woman with iron-gray hair emerged. She might be eighty years old, Quist thought, but she walked like an athlete. She waved and called out, "Wally!"

From somewhere behind the house came a chorus of barking and howling. The lady of the house was on the move, and her orphaned dogs let her know they were there.

"Wally! You look marvelous!" Maggie Nolan said. She put her arms around the young man and gave him a hug. Then she turned. "You must be Julian Quist. Jerry Collins called me to let me know you two were on your way up here. I was playing one of your records, Wally."

"We heard," Wally said. "You look marvelous, too, Miss Nolan."

" 'Maggie' to both of you," the elderly woman said. "That song may just help make you mayor of Bridgetown, Wally. People remember the old rat pack. They all turned out better than the 'good guys.' Come on in."

Quist thought he'd never seen a living room to match the one in Maggie Nolan's house. He knew valuable antiques when he saw them, and these had been chosen with exquisite taste. The painting over the fireplace mantel was unmistakably a portrait of Maggie when she was much younger, painted with all the bizarre caricature techniques of Pablo Picasso. It had to be an original by that famous artist, priceless.

"It's early in the day for serious drinking," Maggie said. "But a little white wine on the rocks? Or some iced coffee?"

"Conversation is what we want most of all," Wally said.

"Will I support your campaign for mayor of Bridgetown?" Maggie asked. "Up to the hilt, Wally. Count on it."

"What do you think Wally's chances are?" Quist asked.

A little muscle rippled along Maggie's jaw. This woman was a fighter, Quist thought. "Not good, but not impossible," she said.

"Your assessment of the situation would be helpful, Miss Nolan," Quist said.

She smiled at him. " 'Maggie,' please." She hesitated a moment. "I know this town inside out," she said finally. "I know just how the machinery is ticking inside Mark Foreman's head, and Seymour Sloan's, and Greg Martin's—and others. Is your reason for running what you say it is, Wally? You want to make a childhood dream of yours and your sister's come true? They don't really believe that, and neither do I."

"What do you think his reason is?" Quist asked.

"To nail Martha's killer," Maggie said.

"Of course that's never out of his mind," Quist said.

"He doesn't believe the accepted story that it was some kind of sex maniac. The big shots here in Bridgetown know it wasn't a sex maniac, and I'd bet all my worldly goods that it wasn't. Martha was going to blow the whistle on the big boys, and they had to stop her."

"You think that and you've never said so in public?" Quist asked.

"I have no proof," Maggie said. "They would laugh at me at first, but then if people started to believe me there'd be a short circuit in my house, or something, and it would burn to the ground. Wally has guessed the way. Get into power and you'd get them cold—not for murder, perhaps, but for the crimes Martha unearthed and for which she had to be silenced. That's the way it is, isn't it, Wally?"

Wally glanced at Quist. It had been thoroughly understood between them that there'd be no whisper of the real motive behind Wally's candidacy. Now, here in the first hours, this woman had laid it right out on the table.

"You know, Wally, and I know, and I suspect Mr. Quist knows, that if the big boys are convinced of Wally's real goal, he not only won't get elected, he might find himself involved in some kind of fatal accident. I certainly wouldn't suggest it because I might find I was accident-prone, too. And so might you, Mr. Quist, if they thought you were heading Wally toward a win."

Neither man spoke. Maggie Nolan's smile was grim. "I'm right, aren't I, Wally, about your real motive?"

Quist spoke before Wally could. "Let's put it this way, Maggie. Wally's reasons for running are what he says they are—to make an old dream of his and his sister's come true. Of course, if he won, he'd certainly check back on all the investigations into Martha's murder. But your 'big boys' have had time to erase any possible lead to a political crime—if there was one."

"Maybe, maybe not," Maggie said.

"You know something they can't cover?" Wally asked, leaning toward the older woman.

"Not yet," Maggie said. "The death of your sister wasn't a one-man job, Wally. I don't mean by that that more than one man was involved in her actual murder. But that one man was hired by the big shots at Manchester Arms and their political allies. Track him down and you've only got the 'gun' that killed her. The real killers are walking around town, free as birds."

"So I'm after a gang of conspirators, not one man?" Wally asked.

"And they will cover their gunman, and they will defeat you in an election, Wally, unless you can come up with a miracle."

Wally glanced at Quist. "I can come up with a pretty substantial sum of money for someone who might want to talk," he said.

"Unless he's a dummy, that man would know he'd never live to spend the money if he decided to talk," Maggie said. "You don't double-cross the powers-that-be and live to spend the money."

"Tough as that?" Quist asked.

"*Tougher* than that if it's necessary," Maggie said. "Let the idea circulate that you're really out to solve a crime, not fulfill a childhood dream, and you're over your heads in quicksand."

"It seems to me," Quist said, "that if the local voters were convinced that a nice and much-liked local girl had been murdered by the town big shots, they'd be apt to support her brother, out to get them, a lot more quickly than they'd work to make a romantic Horatio Alger dream come true."

"Would you put your hand down in front of a buzz saw just to help a kid with a grudge against the buzz saw operator?" Maggie asked. "Let me tell you, Julian, if Wally's true motive starts to circulate, he couldn't get elected dogcatcher, let alone mayor. Persuade people of a romantic dream and a lot of old buzzards like me will vote for Wally because they think it's 'sweet.' They understand dreams. Even hint to them that crime is involved and they suddenly won't be able to hear what you're saying. Too dangerous, and they won't really understand how it could be. I can sell a dream to a lot of people in this town, but a hunt for a murderer had better be left alone. Your problem, Wally, is to get elected. Cops and robbers comes after that, if you do succeed."

Quist gave the elderly woman his most charming smile. "So, lay out a campaign for us, Maggie," he said.

Maggie gave a quick, affirmative nod of her gray head, crossed over to a desk in the corner, and came back with a pad and a ballpoint pen. "There are two angles you have to consider in this," she said. "There's the public game you play, and the private game you play." She wrote down two headings on her pad. "Wally has to play the public game. Women's clubs, social gatherings that I can arrange for you, public gatherings of the very young and the very old—all sentimentalists. Your main weapon will be your guitar, to accompany you in song. If you're going to be mayor, Wally, you'll have to sing your way into the office. Along with that will go the sweet, heartwarming story of how you and your sister grew up here in Bridgetown, poor, disadvantaged. How you dreamed of finding a way to get yourselves loved and admired by the home folks. How you made it with your singing, Wally, and how Martha made it by becoming private secretary to Mark Foreman, the most important man in town. How, after Martha's tragic death, you dream of going one step higher on the Bridgetown ladder, to honor her and to make her proud and happy that your dream has come true. Not one word, ever, about revenge, or any suggestion that Martha wasn't killed by a sex maniac. Sweetness, light, and love! I suppose some of Julian's people can write the script for you." Her smile was sardonic. "It should be the soap opera to end all soap operas."

"I have a lady who can write a script that will bring tears to your eyes," Quist said, thinking of Lydia Morton.

"Good," Maggie said. "If you can sell that, you can come close—if. And it's a big 'if.' "

"And that 'if' is—?" Quist asked.

"If, privately, you can convince the powers-that-be that it's the truth. They might even decide to let you win, counting on being able to control you once you're in. Make them look more like Santa Claus than the devil."

"And I start where?" Quist asked.

"You start with Mark Foreman, the president of Manchester Arms. He was Martha's boss, and the logical person to ask for help for Wally—if he were an honest man."

"I think you've hit the nail right on the head," Quist said.

"Play it cool with Mark Foreman, Julian. Let him ask you. Don't ask him. That way you'll know what he wants to know. Check back with me in a couple of days and I'll have set up some appearances for Wally."

"She could be a great help," Wally said as he and Quist started to drive back down into town.

"She could also be right," Quist said. "There are a lot of young people who grew up with you here in Bridgetown?"

"Quite a few."

"I think you should circulate with them, get them lined up on your side, while I try on Mark Foreman for size," Quist said.

"Shouldn't I go with you to see Foreman?" Wally asked. "I knew him when Martha was working for him, and I saw a lot of him after—after Martha was killed."

"To tell you the truth, Wally, I'm not sure you're a good enough actor to hide what you're really thinking from him. I agree with Miss Nolan. Confirm his suspicions about your reason for running and we might as well be trying to sell tea in China."

"You're the boss," Wally said.

"Let's keep it that way," Quist said, "until you think I'm not doing a good job for you."

From his hotel room Quist called Manchester Arms and asked for Mark Foreman. He got a secretary who asked who he was and what he wanted. When he explained he was put on hold. A couple of moments later a strong male voice came on the line.

"Mr. Quist? This is Mark Foreman."

"I wondered if you could spare me a few minutes of your time. I wanted to talk to you—"

"About Wally Best's political hopes," Foreman interrupted. "I know who you are, Mr. Quist, and how highly you rate in your profession. Name the time."

"This afternoon?"

"I'll be here and expecting you," Foreman said.

The receptionist at Manchester Arms was also expecting Quist when he arrived at the giant plant down by the river. An office boy took him up to the third floor in a noiseless elevator. Mark Foreman's office was large, airy, looking down on the river, but there was nothing fancy about it—two desks, a typewriter, dictating machines, filing cabinets. A plain-looking young woman, her short brown hair worn in a Dutch bob, greeted him.

"I'm Betsy, Mr. Foreman's secretary," she said. "Mr. Foreman's been alerted that you were on your way up. He should be here any minute."

"Thank you," Quist said.

"Of course I know why you're here, Mr. Quist." She gave Quist a sly smile, as if they were two kids conspiring to raid the cookie jar. "You're working to promote Wally Best's campaign."

"That's the story."

"Mr. Foreman says Wally must be serious or he wouldn't have hired someone like you to help him," Betsy said.

"Promoting people and their causes is my business," Quist said, "just as making guns is yours."

Betsy giggled. "Mercy, I don't make guns, Mr. Quist. I just take Mr. Foreman's dictation and protect him from crank phone calls." Then her face sobered. "I don't know Wally. I'm not a local girl. Mr. Foreman brought me here from the Chicago office after—after Martha was lost. But, of course, I'm a fan of his, own a lot of his records, watch him on TV. There's something I wish you'd tell him when you see him."

"I can try."

"Tell him I appreciate what a marvelous person his sister must have been. She wasn't expecting to die. She had no reason to prepare her office for a stranger. Yet when I came here there wasn't a thing out of place in this office, nothing that had to be explained, nothing I couldn't find instantly if Mr. Foreman asked for it. It was a model of secretarial organization. I'd like Wally to know how much I appreciated it—and how sorry I am for him in his loss."

"Of course I'll tell him," Quist said.

A rear door in the office opened, and a man came in. He was big and broad-shouldered with deep-set black eyes, curly black hair only slightly sprinkled with gray, and a square jaw that suggested a kind of special toughness. He was wearing dark blue work overalls and a pale blue work shirt opened at a corded neck, and he was pulling off a pair of grease-stained work gloves.

"Sorry to keep you waiting, Quist. I'm Mark Foreman." He smiled. "You expected the president of Manchester Arms to be wearing a winged collar and a bow tie? I spend a lot of my time down where the work gets done. That's where I started thirty years ago. That's what I know best."

Quist braced himself against what he knew was going to be an iron handshake.

"Sit," Foreman said, indicating an armchair beside his desk. He turned to Betsy. "See if you can rustle us up some coffee, Betsy." He glanced at Quist. "Something else you'd prefer?"

"Coffee, black, would be fine," Quist said.

Foreman sat in the upholstered swivel chair behind his desk. "You're here to talk about Wally Best, of course. I must say I was surprised to hear that Julian Quist Associates had agreed to handle his campaign for mayor of Bridgetown. I find it hard to believe that a firm of your standing would be involved in trying to sell something that can't be sold."

"Selling mother love has always been a pushover," Quist said. "The love of siblings for each other may run a close second."

"But the mayoralty of Bridgetown can't be important in your scheme of things," Foreman said.

"You're overlooking something, Mr. Foreman," Quist said. "Ten years ago we launched Wally Best as a country singer, built him up from a green kid without two nickels to rub against each other, and turned him into a multi-million-dollar business success. When he came to us with this idea, we couldn't turn him down, no matter how unlikely the project was. He was an old professional friend."

Foreman's eyes narrowed. "That much money, huh?"

"I don't suppose it's a secret. Huge record sales, concerts, they add up."

"It would be a joke—except for the money he might be willing to spend," Foreman said.

"Oh, he's willing to spend," Quist said. He grinned. "He's hired me, hasn't he?"

"You don't have to get him elected to get paid. You just have to make him look good," Foreman said, his forehead furrowed by a deep frown.

"He's the best at what he is, a singer, entertainer. I take it your man, Greg Martin, doesn't sing."

Foreman's laugh exploded. "He can't even carry a tune. But he knows how to run a city."

"The way you want it run?"

"We are the city of Bridgetown, the source of its economy. We're not kids playing games, Quist. The chief officer of this town knows which side his bread is buttered on. So do the people."

"Then you have nothing to worry about from the Rat Pack Lover," Quist said.

"I hear a slogan going around," Foreman said. " 'Best is best for Bridgetown.' "

"One of my people invented it," Quist said. "Rather good, don't you think?"

Foreman brought the flat of his hand down hard on his desk. "This isn't a game, Quist! It isn't practical for Manchester Arms to have an amateur running this town."

"From all I hear, there's no way that can happen," Quist said.

"Because we won't let it happen," Foreman said. "No yodeler is going to be allowed to throw roadblocks in our way."

"Why would Wally want to throw roadblocks in your way?"

"If I knew his real reason for running, maybe I could answer that," Foreman said, his whole manner toughening. "The job represents peanuts in money according to his scale of living."

Here it was, Quist thought, the place where he had to begin selling a lie. "A kid's dream," he said. "It would have pleased Martha. He wants to honor her memory."

"Or get even for her," Foreman said.

"I don't understand," Quist said, looking straight at the man across the desk from him. "Get even for what?"

"He thinks the local authorities botched the investigation of Martha's murder."

"Did they?" Quist asked.

"There was nothing much to botch," Foreman said. "Girl left her car to go into a shop. A sex maniac grabbed her, took her away, raped her, strangled her in the process."

"Then waited some days to put the body in the trunk of her car right under the noses of the police?"

"I should have Captain Seaton of our police force brief you on the investigation," Foreman said. "Everyone has asked the same question you ask. Why did the murderer wait days before putting Martha's body in the car trunk, and how could he have managed it right in a police parking lot?"

"And does your man, Seaton, have the answers?"

Foreman shrugged. "Like everything in this case, there's nothing but guesswork, no solid clues. The first guess is an ugly one. Martha's body wasn't in the car when she first turned up missing. It was there nine days later when Wally Best's private investigator looked. We came to think—I was persuaded to believe, let's say—that Martha wasn't killed the night she left her car parked outside the Guardinos' store. She was grabbed by the man we can't identify, taken somewhere, raped and raped again, for a period of several days. Between attacks on her, the killer followed the progress of the case on TV or radio. Eventually, maybe Martha fought too hard; maybe the man just ran out of time. He killed her. As I say, it's an ugly business to contemplate, and let me tell you that if I could get my hands on that son of a bitch, I'd take great pleasure in chopping him into a thousand small pieces. Martha was a very special girl."

"But why risk taking her body back into a police parking lot and putting it in her own car?"

"Best place in the world," Foreman said. "Her car had already been searched. No reason for the police to look there again."

"But how did he get into that parking lot, carrying a body?"

"Other people have asked that, and there's an answer," Foreman said. "That wasn't a parking lot in the regular sense of the word—a place you could leave your car for an hour and then go back and get it. That place was used for impounded cars. You had to go to police headquarters to reclaim your vehicle if it had been towed away. There was a cop guarding the lot, but all he had to do was prevent anyone from driving a car out of the lot without the proper papers. There was only one way a car could be driven out: through the front gate, which was kept closed. There's a little shed by the entrance. It was bitter cold for almost a week. The cop on duty stayed in that shed, in front of an electric heater. No one could drive a car out without getting him to open the gate. He didn't have to watch for anything else. If someone wanted to walk into the lot to see if his car was there, there was nothing but a post-and-rail fence to stop him. The cop stayed warm, and the murderer carried Martha's body in over the fence somewhere and put it in the trunk."

"How did he get the trunk open?"

"The keys were in the car's ignition."

"You mean anyone could walk in and drive away any car?"

Foreman looked impatient. "Only once in a thousand times when the police tow away a car do they find the keys in them. There's no established way for dealing with keys left behind because it almost never happens. So, in this case, they just left the keys in the car." Foreman glanced at his wrist watch. "Any other way I can help you, Quist?"

"Give me your picture of Martha Best," Quist said.

Foreman made a church steeple out of his fingers. "She came to work at Manchester about eight years ago. I'd have to look at the records to give you an exact date. She was in the secretarial pool, filling in for anyone who was out sick or for some other reason. Just exactly four years ago this month—August—my secretary went on vacation and I asked for a girl from the secretarial pool to fill in. I got Martha." Foreman hesitated, moistening his lips with the tip of his tongue. "Good looks, beauty, are really hard to describe, you know? An artist sees it one way, a lover sees it another. For me it's never been classic bone structure, or a sensuous figure, or what-have-you. For me it comes from some kind of light that turns on inside, lights up, shines out. I suppose it's some kind of special energy. That's what makes for beauty in my book. Martha had it. She was so damned alive!" Foreman looked away, fumbling rather uncertainly for a cigarette from the pack on his desk. He finally got the cigarette lighted and took a deep drag from it. "If I wasn't attracted by that, I certainly would have been by the way she did her job. She was super. She transformed what I thought was a pretty well-organized system into perfection. I began to wonder what I was going to do when my regular girl came back from vacation. I—I didn't want to lose Martha. I didn't have to—then. God took care of that. My regular girl was killed in a car accident on the way back from her vacation. So—Martha stayed with me until that February morning when she didn't show up for work."

"You had no difficulties with her, no quarrels?"

Foreman gave Quist a bitter smile. "I'm a man, you know, with a man's impulses. I made the usual pass at an attractive woman. I got a 'No,' but I also got the impression that she wasn't saying 'Never.' I was getting a little impatient when God took a hand again." Foreman shook himself, almost like a dog coming out from a swim. "Enough of that, Quist."

"Asking about Martha is important to me," Quist said. "She's at the very center of Wally's reason for running for mayor of Bridgetown. The murder can't be hidden under a barrel. I need to be able to handle any curves that are thrown at me along the way. Somebody could try to dirty up Martha's reputation. I need to know how to handle those curves."

"You can count on me to help you any way I can if someone takes aim at Martha," Foreman said. "But you can also count on me to make sure you don't get Wally elected!" He stood up and held out his hand. "Now, if you'll excuse me, the day's running away on me."

Chapter Three

The calm before the storm, Quist thought as he left Mark Foreman's office. He had carefully lied to Foreman about Wally Best's real motive for running for office, and Foreman, if what Wally suspected about him was correct, had lied about Martha.

The heat of the August afternoon beat down on the city as Quist walked toward his hotel. He wondered what it had been like that terrible night when Martha had met a killer: a blizzard, bitter cold that had frozen her body solid when it had been left in the trunk of her car. Had the guard in the little gatehouse, sitting huddled by his electric heater, been aware of the conspiracy to hide the body just yards away? Or had he even been part of it, helped dispose of Martha's remains or been ordered to keep his eyes and ears shut? Quist knew that he had to make a decision. Would he simply devote himself to an election campaign or would he, in the process, try to unmask a killer or killers? Wally would have no chance to play detective during the campaign. He would be watched every step of the way. Every question he might ask would be carried back to the person or people concerned. Wally's only chance was to wait two-and-a-half months for the outcome at the polls, and then, if by some miracle he was elected, have a chance to dig into records. Even then, the truth about Martha could stay hidden. Wally might stumble onto some of the facts that Martha had unearthed and that had cost her her life. He might be able to bring criminal charges against the men for business crimes they'd committed and never come close to the truth about his sister. Quist's gut feeling, as he headed for the hotel, was that Foreman and his allies were too solidly entrenched in Bridgetown for Wally to have a chance in the election, no matter how clever his campaign. He could hear Dan Garvey warning him: "Stay out of it! You can only get clobbered!" They could, Quist told himself, devote two-and-a-half months to the election, staying away from the investigation of Martha's death to reduce the determination of the opposition, lose, and be nowhere.

The answer, Quist concluded as he approached the hotel, was for Wally to play it loose, singing his way around town and talking between songs about honoring his late sister. Foreman and his pals would be watching Wally every step of the way, but they just might not pay attention to Quist until he'd managed to get his foot in the door. Whatever his friend Dan Garvey might think, Quist decided that he must take whatever opportunity he had to track down Martha's killer, camouflaged by the election campaign.

He picked up the key to his room at the hotel's front desk and took the elevator up to the seventh floor, where his room was located. He unlocked the door, stepped in, and froze.

The room was a shambles. Clothes had been taken out of the closet and scattered on the floor and on the bed; bureau drawers had been pulled out, contents tossed around; his suitcase had been opened, the lining ripped apart. But more important, a woman, wearing a maid's outfit, was lying on the floor beside the bed, a pool of blood surrounding a blond head. If she was alive, Quist couldn't tell it from where he stood.

Quist went quickly to the woman and knelt beside her. He couldn't detect that she was breathing, or feel even a faint pulse at her wrist. He slipped an arm under her and started to lift her. The wound at the back of her head was a dreadful violence. He lowered her and went to the phone. He needed an ambulance, the house doctor, the police. There was a clean bath towel lying near the body, and he lifted the woman a few inches again and placed the towel under her head.

Moments after he started making the telephone calls, there was a sharp knock at the door and a man burst in without waiting for an invitation.

"I'm Doug Melton, the house detective," the man said. Then his face twisted in sudden pain. "My God, it's Sue Wilson." He ran to the woman's body and knelt beside her. He called out to her. "Sue! Sue, it's Doug!"

"I couldn't detect any signs of life," Quist said.

Melton turned his head, still clutching at the woman's hands. "What the hell happened here?"

"I don't know," Quist said. "I just came in and found things the way you see them."

"Who are you?"

"I'm Julian Quist. I'm registered in this room. For your information I haven't touched anything except that towel. It was lying nearby and I put it under her head."

"The weapon?"

"I haven't started to look for anything," Quist said. "I just called for help. There should be an ambulance soon."

Melton had left the door to the room open. Another man came in, carrying a small black bag.

"I'm Keeler," the man said. "The house doctor."

The doctor went over to the woman and knelt beside her. "Jesus!" he said when he saw the wound at the back of her head.

"She's not breathing, Doc," Melton said.

"Lucky if she ever does again," the doctor said. He opened his bag, prepared some kind of hypodermic, and drove the needle into the woman's arm. Then he let her arm fall and stood up. "What happened?"

Quist told his story. "I found her like this, not ten minutes ago."

"It happened a lot longer ago than that," the doctor said. "She's been bleeding and bleeding for a long time." He paused, then looked at Quist. "You found her robbing your room and you hit her?"

"Don't be a damn fool, Doc," Melton said. "She wouldn't have been robbing this room. Sue was bringing in some clean towels; regular routine. There are a couple there on the floor and the one Quist put under her head."

"She wasn't just punched in the head, you know," the doctor said. "This wound was inflicted by the classic 'blunt instrument'—a gun butt, a hammer, an iron wrecking bar." He glanced at Melton. "You searched this man?"

"No," Melton said. He moved toward Quist. "Take it easy, buster."

"Help yourself," Quist said, and held his arms out from his sides.

Melton patted him over and turned away. "Clean," he said.

More people came into the room, obviously the ambulance crew. Keeler took the ambulance doctor aside while two attendants lifted the woman onto a stretcher, covered her with a sheet, and carried her out. Dr. Keeler went with them.

"We stay here till the cops come," Melton said to Quist.

"You sounded as if you know the girl," Quist said.

"Know her!" Melton almost shouted. "She's my lady, my woman!"

"I'm sorry," Quist said.

"So help me, Quist, if you're not telling me all you know—" The threat wasn't put into words.

"I've told you exactly what happened," Quist said. "I got my key at the desk, came up here, let myself in, and found her just as you saw her."

"You have any conversation with her since you checked in? She's the maid on this floor."

"Never laid eyes on her till I found her. I just checked in this morning. I never saw a maid, had no reason to want to see one. I went out on business. When I came back a couple of hours later—" Quist spread his hands in a helpless gesture.

"What would the thief have been looking for?" a voice asked from the doorway.

A uniformed policeman and a man in plain clothes were standing there.

"Hi, Doug," the plainclothesman said as he came into the room. "I talked with Doc Keeler down by the ambulance. Looks bad, according to him."

"This is Captain Walter Seaton, Bridgetown Homicide," Melton said, indicating the man in plain clothes. "This is Julian Quist, the guy who's registered in this room, Walter."

The name rang a bell with Quist. Captain Seaton was the cop who had been in charge of investigating Martha Best's murder.

"I happen to know who you are, Quist," Seaton said. "You're a public relations man for Wally Best and his crazy campaign."

"I happen to know who you are, Captain," Quist said. "You're the cop who couldn't find Martha Best's killer."

Seaton's thin lips moved in an ugly smile. "Okay, wise guy!" he said. "Maybe this one won't be so tough. What could a thief have been looking for here?"

"You've got me," Quist said. "Something worth pawning, I suppose."

"I'm not a kindergarten cop," Seaton said. "This character wasn't looking for something that was just lying around loose. The pockets of your clothes turned inside out, everything else shaken out, the lining of your suitcase cut open—this guy was looking for something he had reason to believe you had hidden here, something not too big to carry in a pocket. Cutting up the lining of that suitcase suggests drugs or jewelry."

"Your police lab should be able to answer that one for you," Quist said. "But if it will save you time, let me assure you there were no drugs, no jewels, nothing of any real value."

"You checked to make sure nothing's gone?" Seaton asked.

"When I got here there was a woman who needed help," Quist said. "I checked on her, telephoned for an ambulance, for the house doctor, for you. I haven't checked on anything because there wasn't anything to take. Extra suit—it's there on the bed. Raincoat and hat—there on the floor. Shirts, handkerchiefs, socks, underwear—I'd have to count, but it looks like everything is here." Quist patted at his jacket pockets. "Everything I have of any value is on me: watch, wallet with credit cards, driver's license, blank checks. I only planned to spend a night, perhaps two, this time in town. Didn't bring anything that would carry me beyond that."

"I'll want to check everything for fingerprints," Seaton said. "Don't touch anything until it's done. Where's your client, Wally Best?"

"He went to see friends. We were to meet back here for lunch. He has a room a couple of doors down and across the hall—number seventy-six."

"What friends?"

"Young people he grew up with here," Quist said. "I haven't gotten to know names yet. Incidentally, Dr. Keeler estimated that Sue Wilson was attacked more than an hour ago. I have an alibi for that time, Captain. I was with a friend of yours."

"Friend of mine?"

"I was with Mark Foreman in his office at Manchester Arms."

A nerve twitched along the line of Seaton's jaw. "Trying to get his vote for Wally Best?" He chuckled at his own joke.

"Never mind votes," Wally Best said. He'd walked in from the hall. "I've got something else for you, Seaton." He knew the policeman from the bitter past. "I see someone's given Julian a going-over. Want to have a look at my room?"

"Why?"

"Same deal," Wally said. "Turned upside down. Looking for what, for God's sake?"

"No dead bodies, I hope," Seaton said.

Wally looked puzzled. Quist told him about Sue Wilson.

"My God, Julian. I know Sue. She was in my class in high school! She's dead?"

"We think so," Quist said. "There's been no official word from the hospital yet."

"But why?"

"She was making a routine delivery of towels," Melton said. "Let herself in with the housekeeper's key and must have caught the thief in the act."

Seaton had walked over to the door of the room. "No indication this door was forced," he said. "How did the thief get in?"

"Key," Melton said.

"Or Quist left the door unlocked when he went out," Seaton said.

"There's no way to leave it unlocked," Melton said. "Close the door and it locks itself."

"So someone released the catch on the lock, earlier," Seaton said.

"Take a look at it," Melton said. "There's no catch to release. Close the door and it's locked. Guy who got in here had to have had a key from somewhere."

"Housekeeper's room on this floor?" Seaton suggested.

"Sue had that key," Melton said. "She was wearing it on a ribbon around her neck when I went to her. Standard practice when the maids are carrying stuff. She let herself in, evidently found the guy here tearing apart Quist's room, and was slugged to keep her from sounding an alarm."

"Where else could the thief have gotten a key?" Seaton asked. "Quist just checked in this morning. It wasn't something the guy could have planned. He wouldn't know what room Quist would be assigned. Or did you make this reservation well in advance, Quist?"

"We didn't make a reservation at all," Quist said. "Wally said there'd be half a dozen places to choose from when we got here. We stopped at Bridgetown House first because it was closest to the center of things. They had a couple of rooms and we took them."

"But people have known for some days you'd be turning up here," Seaton said. "It's been in the papers, on television."

"True," Quist said. "But no one could have known that we were going to stay here in Bridgetown House, because we didn't know ourselves until we got here."

"You may be used to walking around unnoticed, Quist," Seaton said, "but Wally can't move an inch in this town without being noticed and watched. Hundreds of people would have known a minute after he registered at the front desk." Seaton turned to the house detective. "If it wasn't the housekeeper's key, where else could the thief have gotten one?"

Doug Melton moistened his lips. "Two places," he said. "The safe in my office, and the vault in the manager's office."

"A key for every door? He'd need two to get into two rooms?"

Melton shook his head. "Not quite that complicated," he said. "I have master keys—one key that will unlock every room on this floor, another that will unlock every door on six, another that will take care of eight—and so on."

"So he got the key that will open the doors on this floor," Seaton said.

"I don't think so," Melton said.

"How do you know? You don't sit on those keys like a mother hen on her eggs."

"But nobody gets one without opening the safe in my office. I'm the only one who knows how to do that without setting off an alarm."

"The manager's vault?"

"The same situation."

Seaton indulged in his sour smile. "So either you or the manager is the thief," he said.

"I'm not laughing," Melton said.

"So, maybe I wasn't being funny," Seaton said. "Let's go have a look at those master keys."

"Aren't you interested in what happened in my room?" Wally Best asked.

Seaton turned to the uniformed cop, who hadn't spoken during all of this. "When the fingerprint crew arrives, have them go over everything in this room, and everything in Best's room. That's number—?"

"Seventy-six," Wally said.

"Let's go look for that master key," Seaton said to Melton.

Melton shook his head. "I've got to get the final answer on Sue," he said. "Damn it, man, she's my girl! She's got a mother who has to be told."

"We can check on your master key on your way to the hospital," Seaton said.

Quist and Wally were left alone with the uniformed cop, who stood by the door, stone-faced.

"What's this all about, Julian?" Wally asked. "Sue Wilson! It's hard to believe. I used to date her when we were teenagers."

"You have a chance to check on anything that might be missing from your room?" Quist asked.

"I just brought overnight stuff," Wally said. "Only thing of real value in the room was my guitar. I examined that. It wasn't damaged, but it had been moved from where I left it."

Quist was silent for a moment. "When I first walked in and saw this," he said finally, "I assumed the girl had caught some ordinary hotel thief at work. But then, when you came in with the news about your room—"

"So the thief was working this floor," Wally said.

Quist shook his head slowly. "I don't think so. The minute we signed the register in the lobby, the whole damn town knew we were here and why."

"Why?"

"To get you elected mayor," Quist said. "Somebody was looking for something specific."

"What?"

"Evidence of some kind. Evidence that you or I might have that would involve someone in Martha's murder, or some other crime the killer committed. Mark Foreman and his friends aren't going to buy your story, you know. They have to make sure just how dangerous you are to them. You're going to have to count on being under their microscope for the next couple of months."

"I wish to God we had evidence," Wally said.

Quist's face hardened. "We're going to find it, boy. At least I'm going to find it while you play the lovable Rat Pack Lover for the general public—and Foreman and company."

"Did Foreman give you any kind of a lead?"

"No. He just promised me he wouldn't let Martha be bad-mouthed during the campaign, and that he wasn't about to let you get elected."

"So where do we go from here?"

"We play the election game and keep our noses to the ground," Quist said.

There were voices at the door. The fingerprint crew had arrived.

Anna Clark, the housekeeper on the seventh floor of Bridgetown House, a motherly woman in her late fifties, was in shock when she encountered Quist and Wally in the hall outside their rooms. The fingerprint crew had ordered the two men out of their rooms until everything had been checked and worked over.

Mrs. Clark didn't need an introduction to know who the two men were.

"I just can't believe it!" Anna Clark said, without any preamble.

"Believe what?" Quist asked.

"The word's just come from the hospital. Sue Wilson didn't make it! She's dead! Forgive me, Wally and Mr. Quist, I'm Anna Clark, the housekeeper for this floor." She shook her head from side to side. "It's hard to believe that only a little more than an hour ago, I ordered Sue to check out the towel supply in your two rooms. I never dreamed I was sending her to her death! I don't believe it now! I sent her!"

"You can't blame yourself, Mrs. Clark," Quist said. "You sent her on a routine chore. You had no reason to think—"

"Maybe I did," Anna Clark interrupted. "I got a call from the front office saying that you'd signed into seventy-six, Wally. Your manager or whatever—you, Mr. Quist—were to be in seventy-one. Mr. Simmons, the manager, said half the celebrity hunters in the county would be jamming up onto my floor to get a glimpse of Wally Best, get his autograph, try to snip off a lock of his hair. I remembered how it was when Frank Sinatra was a guest here years ago. Mr. Simmons wanted me to be sure there were extra towels, everything in order. So I sent Sue. She was on duty. I gave her the master key and sent her off with extra towels."

"If she'd come to my room while I was there, I'd have known her," Wally said. "We went to high school together. I used to date her!"

"I know," Mrs. Clark said. "She was excited about seeing you again. But she went to Mr. Quist's room first, seventy-one. It was the first on her way. She must have caught someone in the act!"

"She had the master key hung on a ribbon around her neck," Quist said.

"Routine again," Mrs. Clark said. "If a maid is going into a room or rooms, I give her that master key. She wears it on that ribbon so that her hands are free for whatever she has to do."

"Just that one key?" Quist asked.

"There are only six rooms in this section—then the open courtyard—and seven north, which is on the other side of the court. Different housekeeper on the north side. I have five, six, seven, and eight on this south side—twenty-four rooms in all, four master keys."

"Any one of the master keys open all twenty-four rooms?" Quist asked.

Mrs. Clark shook her head. "A different master for each six rooms."

"Then the thief had to have the use of the key Sue Wilson was wearing when I found her," Quist said.

"No way," Mrs. Clark said. "I had the key till I gave it to Sue."

"Where else could he have gotten a master key?" Quist asked.

Mrs. Clark hesitated. "Mr. Simmons, the manager, has duplicates of all the masters in his vault. Doug Melton, the house detective, keeps copies in his safe."

"Then the thief had to get his key from one of those places."

"Not without Mr. Simmons or Doug Melton knowing," Mrs. Clark said.

Quist let it ride for a moment. "But it was no secret that Wally was in seventy-six and I was in seventy-one. Mr. Simmons told you—and how many others? Having Wally Best here as a guest wasn't a secret, wasn't supposed to be a secret."

"But the news could only just have started to spread," Mrs. Clark added. "You'd only just been assigned to those rooms, and you both went out as soon as you'd taken your luggage in."

"But there are still other keys besides the masters," Wally said. "The ones that were given to us at the desk. We left our keys at the front desk when we went out. The thief could have gotten one of those and used it."

"And stopped to return them after he'd killed Sue Wilson?" Quist asked. "They were where they should have been when we came back. I got mine, let myself into my room, and found Sue. You got yours, let yourself into your room, and found it had been ransacked. The thief knew which rooms we had, got the right keys for them—returned them?"

Mrs. Clark frowned. "When someone famous like Wally checks in, the desk clerk and the switchboard operators don't give out the number of their room. That's to keep the famous person from being bothered."

"But those clerks, the switchboard operators, knew which rooms we had."

"So one of them could be the thief—and the killer," Wally said.

"Or allied with the thief and killer. Tells the killer which rooms, gets the keys for him, replaces them when the job is done."

Mrs. Clark's eyes widened. "You think someone on the hotel staff—?"

"What else?" Quist asked. "Tell me, Mrs. Clark, who owns Bridgetown House?"

"Why—why Manchester Arms owns it, like everything else important in town," the woman said.

Quist glanced at Wally. "Do we need any more?"

Wally shook his head. "It was pure chance that we came here. I suggested it because it was close to the center of everything—and the best in town."

"Would you like to bet that we could have gotten rooms any place that wasn't owned by Mark Foreman and Company?" Quist asked. "We had to be where they could watch every move we made."

The elevator doors at the far end of the hall slid open and Captain Seaton and another man came toward them.

"Mr. Simmons, the manager," Mrs. Clark said to Quist, in what was almost a whisper.

Simmons was a short, square little man with a shiny bald head. He came up to Quist and Wally. "I'm Luke Simmons, the manager," he said. "I can't tell you how sorry I am about all this mess."

"Is 'mess' your word for murder, Mr. Simmons?" Quist asked.

"You know about the Wilson girl?"

"Mrs. Clark just told us."

"Bad news travels fast," Captain Seaton said. "Fractured skull, brain damage. Maybe she's lucky she didn't make it."

"I'd like to assign you and Wally to different rooms," Simmons said. "Be pleasanter for you, and the police will be concentrating on this floor."

"Maybe we should go somewhere else," Wally said.

"Oh, I hope you won't do that," Simmons said. "We'd like to be able to make it up to you. There's a two-bedroom suite on the tenth floor that's available. You'd be together. I'll have Mrs. Clark pack up your things when the police are through, have any clothes that need pressing attended to. Let us do that for you."

Wally glanced at Quist.

"We accept," Quist said. He turned to the homicide man. "You come up with any answers about the key or keys, Seaton?"

"Mr. Simmons's keys are where they should be," Seaton said. "Doug Melton's keys are in his safe. Of course, they could have been taken and replaced."

"By—?"

Simmons indulged in a hollow little laugh. "The obvious answer to that, Mr. Quist, is me or Doug Melton. Let me assure you that it wasn't me, and I trust Melton right down to the end of the line."

"You dreamed up a motive, Captain?" Quist asked.

Seaton's smile was sardonic. "In this day and age, people like Wally Best get special attention. I remember we had a movie star here once, and people cut pieces off his suit, hungry for any kind of souvenir. I think that's why your rooms were searched; something to remember Wally by."

"And murder to avoid being caught?" Quist asked incredulously.

Seaton shrugged. "People react kind of crazy when they're caught in a tight spot."

"All the guy had to do when Sue Wilson caught him in my room was run for it. He didn't have to kill her—unless—"

"Unless what?" Seaton asked.

"Unless she knew him, could finger him," Quist said.

"You're suggesting one of our staff?" Simmons asked.

"Seems likely," Quist said. "Someone who knew where to get a key, could replace it later. Why search my room? I'm not a famous person like Wally. There wouldn't be any souvenirs of any importance in my room."

"You're Wally's promoter," Seaton said. "This guy didn't find anything in Wally's room he wanted, thought he'd try yours—for something of Wally's."

"Let me take you up to ten," Simmons said, "and settle you in. Mrs. Clark will get your things to you as quickly as possible."

"Why not?" Quist said.

The tenth-floor suite was a comfortable setup, with a living room, two bedrooms, and a connecting bath. There was nothing noticeable about the décor: a couch, a couple of comfortable chairs, a small writing desk.

"I hope you'll find this pleasant," Simmons said. "Fine view of the town and the river. Now, can I order you some coffee or something? Your favorite liquor from the bar? On the house, of course."

"We'll wait until we can settle in," Quist said.

"Just call room service and order what you want—on me," Simmons said. "Mrs. Clark will be as quick as she can with your things."

"One question," Quist said. It was aimed at Captain Seaton, who was standing to one side with a satisfied little smile moving his thin lips.

"Fire away," Seaton said.

"What about the keys to this room?" Quist asked.

"Same as downstairs," Simmons said, answering the question. "Housekeeper on this floor, Doug Melton, me."

"So we aren't any safer here than we were downstairs," Quist said. "Guy who knows how to get a master key can still get it."

"Oh, come on, Quist!" Seaton said. "You don't think we'll let ourselves be had twice running, do you? We'll have someone stationed outside in the hall, watching this suite around the clock. No one who isn't entitled is going to come snooping around here."

"Remember, whatever you want or need is on us," Simmons said.

"We'll check back with you in a little while," Seaton said.

The manager and the detective walked out into the hall. The door closed behind them and automatically locked. Wally started to speak, but Quist made a silencing gesture with his finger, walked over to the writing desk, and wrote something on hotel letterhead. He handed it to Wally.

"Keep it casual, Wally," the note read. "They were so eager for us to be here, the suite may be bugged."

Wally nodded. Quist held his cigarette lighter to the piece of paper and dropped it into an ashtray on the desk. It burned to a black ash.

"This looks like a comfortable place," Quist said, loud and clear.

"Sure does," Wally said. "Look, I'd like to check with Sue Wilson's mother to see if I can do anything to help. Mrs. Wilson used to make the greatest chocolate chip cookies—long ago when I was dating Sue."

"I'll go with you," Quist said, still making a cautioning gesture for silence. He was moving quickly around the room, trying to find some indication that the place was bugged.

Without any further conversation, they left the suite, went down in the elevator, and were instantly surrounded by a small army of people, all suddenly delighted to see Wally Best. Simmons was in the center of the group, talking to a distinguished-looking gray-haired man wearing a seersucker summer suit and a navy blue sport shirt.

"Someone you ought to know, Wally," Simmons said. "This is Greg Martin. You'll be sharing the spotlight with him for the next couple of months. Greg's running for mayor on the Republican ticket."

Martin's smile was relaxed. "One thing I can't compete with, Wally, is your singing." He held out his hand. There was a chorus of "You can say that again" from the happy onlookers.

"I don't remember you, Mr. Martin," Wally said. "I grew up here, thought I knew everyone of importance in town—at least by sight."

"You were away getting famous when I came to Bridgetown," Martin said. He turned. "You must be Julian Quist."

"Guilty," Quist said. He accepted the offered handshake. It was firm but not torturing. A typical business executive, he thought. The outward mask was friendly and cordial. The real man was not so obvious.

"I was shocked to hear from Simmons what's been happening here," Martin said. "I understand you knew the girl. Sue Wilson."

"High school," Wally said. "I'm on my way to see if I can be of any help to her mother."

"Manchester Arms has already sent someone," Martin said. "They feel responsible since it happened here in a place they own."

"A vote getter," Quist said.

Martin's smile widened. "As you are well aware, Mr. Quist, since you're on your way to offer help yourselves. But that's a little cynical, don't you think? Decent thing for Manchester to do, decent thing for Wally, an old friend, to do. I haven't had a chance to talk to Mark Foreman, but I'm sure he's outraged that this thing could have happened to you, Wally."

"It didn't happen to me," Wally said. "It happened to Sue. It turns out Bridgetown isn't a very safe place for young girls these days. First there was my sister, and now Sue Wilson."

"You don't think the two things are connected, do you?" Martin asked. "One was a sex crime, the other just the unfortunate accident of catching a thief at work."

"Martha worked for Manchester Arms," Wally said. "Sue was killed in a place owned by Manchester Arms. That's a connection, don't you think?"

"A very unfortunate one," Martin said, "but it doesn't mean very much. Almost nothing can happen in this town that doesn't connect up with Manchester in some fashion."

Quist's smile was open. "Including getting elected mayor," he said.

Martin smiled back. "Just remember, I can't sing," he said. "Who knows, that may make Wally and me about even when it comes to getting votes."

Wally was surrounded by eager autograph seekers, and Quist waited for him near the front entrance of the hotel. Two murders, he was thinking, and they were slowly catching up with people who were part of the machine that was possibly—probably—responsible. They were going to have to play it as cool as Greg Martin and Luke Simmons if they were to have any chance of getting at the truth.

When Wally was finally free, they took their car and headed, under Wally's direction, to the house in the lower part of town where Sue Wilson's mother lived. They had been preceded by several cars and a small group of young people, who were now crowded outside the front door. They greeted Wally with enthusiasm. Hometown friends, Quist thought. A young man about Wally's age joined them.

"This is Bobby Shanks," Wally said, introducing Quist to him. "I warn you, Julian, he doesn't like jokes about 'Shanks' mare.' "

"Not interested in any kind of jokes today," Shanks said. Quist noticed that one of the young man's ears was pierced and that he was wearing an earring. "What a hell of a thing, Wally. Do they know any more back at the hotel?"

"Not yet," Wally said. "How is Mrs. Wilson?"

"We don't know," Shanks said. "We haven't seen her yet. Some big shots are with her. Seymour Sloan, Bart Havens."

"Sloan is the chairman of the board at Manchester Arms," Wally told Quist. "Bart Havens is their chief of security." He turned back to Shanks. "Greg Martin told us that Manchester would be offering Mrs. Wilson help."

"But her friends can't get to her," Shanks said. "When we find the son of a bitch who did this . . ." He didn't go on.

The front door opened, and two men came out. Quist didn't have to be told which was which. The sandy-haired man in the Brooks Brothers summer suit would be Sloan; the man with the shaved head and the grim smile, looking like the actor Telly Savalas, would be Havens, the security man. Smiling! These bastards are always smiling, Quist thought.

Seymour Sloan approached Wally. "Nice of you to come out here, Wally," he said. Close up, Quist could smell an expensive shaving lotion. "Mrs. Wilson is pretty badly shaken, as you can imagine. We'll take care of any financial problems she may have, but we can't give her what you can. You were an old friend of Sue's, I understand."

"I used to date Sue," Wally said. "This is Julian Quist. He is—"

"I know who Mr. Quist is and why he's here," Sloan said. "Rough start for a campaign, Mr. Quist."

"Not the kind of advantage we were looking for," Quist said.

"Advantage?" Sloan said, frowning. "I don't follow."

"This happened in Manchester's hotel," Quist said. "A lot of people might decide not to vote for Manchester's candidate."

"Don't worry, Quist," Havens said in a harsh voice. "We'll hang this bastard out to dry long before it's time to go to the polls." His smile returned. "Stay out of trouble, fellows."

Quist and Wally went into the house, followed by the small army of Wally's friends. Grace Wilson was a small dark-haired woman, obviously torn to pieces by what had happened. One look at Wally and she was in his arms, sobbing out of control. There wasn't a sound from anyone else, almost like during a church service. Finally Mrs. Wilson spoke understandable words.

"It—it happened to you first, Wally—now to me! It's hard to believe."

"Let me take you where you can get pulled together," Wally said, and he gently led the woman out of the room.

Quist found himself face to face with Bobby Shanks, Wally's friend. The young man's freckled face was set in a hard mask.

"They were looking for something Wally might have on them, weren't they?" Shanks asked.

"That's a pretty shrewd guess, I think," Quist said.

Shanks pounded a fist into the palm of his hand. "We'll go over those jerks at Manchester Arms with a fine-toothed comb until we solve both these cases," he said.

"We?"

"You know that song of Wally's—'The Rat Pack Lover'? Like Wally, I was one of the pack in the old days. You'd be surprised how sharp we were—and still are! There isn't much about this town we don't know, or can't find out."

"If you and I are right," Quist said, "the people we're after make the guns, and they hold them—right now aimed straight at us."

"So, moving targets aren't easy to hit," Shanks said. "First thing, we've got to make Wally's run for the mayor's job real."

"It's real enough," Quist said.

"It's got to be really real," Shanks said. "We've got to make it happen. Once he's mayor, he's got them behind the eight ball."

"If they see that coming, Wally's in big danger," Quist said.

"Not here in Bridgetown," Shanks said. "The Rat Pack will cover him, night and day. You get him elected, Quist, and we'll keep him safe." He gave Quist a twisted grin. "You just might find yourself in a little trouble if it looks like you're making it, Quist. Don't worry. We'll be right around the corner if you need help."

Wally came back from where he'd taken Sue's mother. He looked as if he'd been hit in the stomach.

"Mrs. Wilson wants you to stick around for a few minutes," he said to his friends. "She wants to thank you for coming."

"Tell her to save her thanks until we bring her the guy who killed Sue," Shanks said. "The body of the guy who killed Sue, on a slab!"

"You got any leads?" Wally asked.

"You and I and anyone else who makes sense knows, at least, who's covering for the killer—probably the same butcher that did for Martha's."

As they waited outside the Wilson house, Quist found himself feeling suddenly old in the presence of Bobby Shanks and his "pack." They were so sure of themselves, so certain that they couldn't fail.

"You and your friends can find yourselves in trouble, too, now that you're on Wally's team, Bobby."

"That's how we grew up—in trouble," Bobby said. "Every time there was a robbery, a store broken into, a fire. 'It's those rat pack kids.' It's always been that way. Nobody ever bothers to check; they just take it for granted. Would you believe they tried to pin Martha Best's murder on us? It was a miracle that it didn't work. The whole pack had hired a bus to go to New York to see a hockey game at Madison Square Garden. A guy who used to be one of us was playing for Boston against the Rangers. That was the night of the blizzard. After the game—which Boston won—our bus driver told us he'd been warned not to try to make the trip back to Bridgetown. Snow, wind, ice—a mess. We got holed up in some fleabag, sleeping on the floor in what they called 'the ballroom.' Point is, every one of us was accounted for. The funny part is the bus was owned by Manchester Arms, the people who wanted to frame one of us. No way out for them. Trains weren't running, highways blocked. No way one of us could have gotten home at the time Martha was attacked. No way one of us could be framed."

"No doubt in your mind that Manchester was responsible for what happened to Martha?"

"She had the goods on them, didn't she? She told Wally. We've been trying ever since to get proof—six months. No luck."

"Not a hint in six months?" Quist asked.

Shanks shook his head. He was an angry young man. "No way we could get to any place there was anything to find—at least until it was too late. Martha's car, for instance. The cops had it tucked away until they'd been able to make sure there was nothing there that would tell us anything. Martha's apartment. We eventually got a key from Wally. So neat you wouldn't believe it. Not a scrap of paper, no letters, no notes of any kind. The cops or somebody had cleaned the apartment out as though she'd never lived there. That's the way the whole town is, Quist. There's no one who ever saw anything, knows anything, heard anything. A sex maniac who skipped town. Period!"

"Not for two or three days till after the night of the blizzard," Quist said. "He had to be here to put the body in the trunk."

"So, obviously, no one left town. They suggest—and the *Journal* supports the theory—it was a stranger passing through, saw a pretty girl on the street, grabbed her, raped her, hung on to her, alive or dead, for a few days, and finally put the body in her car."

"If it was a stranger, how did he know it was her car?"

"Saw her park it."

"So she was raped, according to the coroner."

"That's how it reads, Quist, 'according to the coroner.' That's the way they want it to look, so that's the way they say it was. No disinterested doctor got to examine her—until it was too late."

"Wally got someone?"

"Eventually. The undertaker had removed any traces that could be positive. The coroner is Manchester's man. The undertaker is Manchester's man. The *Journal* is Manchester's paper."

"Captain Seaton?"

Shanks laughed. "The homicide cop? Right in their hip pocket."

"What about Doug Melton, the house detective at the hotel?"

Shanks hesitated. "It's Manchester's hotel, of course. But Doug and Sue were like that!" He crossed two fingers of his right hand. "No way in the world Doug would have killed Sue. He wouldn't have had to. She'd have kept her mouth shut if he'd asked her to. She'd have helped him put the room back in order. He's on Manchester's payroll, by way of the hotel, but he would never have hurt Sue.

"Doug is a local kid," Shanks continued. "We played stickball together in the streets when we were ten years old. He might search someone's room if he got the word, he might slip the wrong person a key if they told him. But kill? I'd have to say no way. Not in him."

"Not if he was caught in the act?"

"By his own girl, who'd go out onto the farthest limb for him? No way."

After a moment Quist pursued it. "So if you were beginning now, Bobby, where would you start?"

"I'd try to get Manchester Arms to hire me for an important job," Shanks said. "No way, however, because I'm a Rat Pack kid. The answer's somewhere on the inside, not the outside. So, what you're trying to do, get Wally elected mayor, is the best answer I've heard so far. But you've got to get him elected before he can make a move."

"You willing to help?" Quist asked.

"Tell us what to do, and we'll do it," Shanks said.

"First of all, you've got to advise *me* what to do," Quist said.

"Don't tell a soul in this town what you're really up to," Shanks said.

"I've already blown that, haven't I?" Quist said. "In this town almost anybody can be bought by Manchester."

A few moments later Wally emerged from the house and he and Quist headed back to their hotel.

"One thing you learn when you grow up poor and suddenly have money," Wally said. "It won't buy you everything you want. Money can't buy back for that lady what she's lost—her daughter."

"Nor, for that matter, your sister, Wally."

Wally nodded, and his voice was bitter when he spoke again. "You think you can just ask and it will be served up for you. You want the touch of a loving hand, and the only hand that touches you belongs to a pickpocket."

Back at the hotel they asked at the desk for the key to their new tenth-floor suite. It was given to them, along with a telephone message for Quist. It was from Dan Garvey in New York. "Call me at the office no matter how late this catches up with you. Emergency. Dan."

Quist tried to imagine what kind of emergency there could be. Julian Quist Associates was handling several other promotions besides Wally's campaign for mayor of Bridgetown, but Dan and Lydia were perfectly competent to make decisions. Something about Wally's campaign that had turned up down there?

It was about six o'clock in the evening when they got to their suite and Quist put in a call to the office in New York. It would normally be closed at this time of day, but a switchboard operator answered promptly.

"Julian Quist here. Is this Norma?"

"Yes, sir. Dan's waiting for your call."

"Murder seems to follow you wherever you go," Garvey said when he answered. "Anything new about the Wilson girl?"

"No. What's wrong, Dan?"

"Lydia's up there with you?"

"Of course not. Why do you ask?"

"You been in touch with her?"

"No. What the hell is this, Dan?"

"When did you last see her?"

"Breakfast," Quist said. "I took off right after that with Wally for here—Bridgetown. What *is* this, Dan?"

Garvey's voice was harsh. "She hasn't shown up here all day, Julian. No message from her. Around eleven in the morning I called your apartment. No answer. A little later I sent Connie over there. Lydia keeps a spare key in her office desk. I thought Lydia might have had an accident, been taken ill. She wasn't there. Nothing out of place, nothing disturbed, no message left for you—or anyone else. We decided that a message must have been fouled up some way. Switchboard girls here swear she never called. I don't like the feel of it, Julian. I thought you should know."

"Well, I should think so. Take me a little over an hour to get down there, Dan."

"I'll be here—unless I get some kind of news. Then somebody will be here."

"It can't be connected with what's going on up here," Quist said.

"Who says it can't?" Garvey asked.

PART 2

Chapter One

Lydia Morton was Quist's world. His work, his job, was fun, challenging, satisfying. Lydia was his life. The sound of her voice, the touch of her hand, the feel of her body beside his were electric, life-giving. His firm could go bankrupt tomorrow and it would be too bad, but he would be able to fight back. If something had happened to Lydia, it would be the end of everything.

He left Wally behind in Bridgetown and headed for New York. Garvey's last words had shaken him. If there was a connection between Lydia's disappearance and Manchester Arms, the feeling of ice around his heart was real. "They will kill and kill again," Garvey had said, early on before Quist had made his decision to help Wally Best. Ugly visions clouded his sight as he raced down the Thruway toward the city. Garvey had asked the right question. "Who says it can't" be connected with Bridgetown? What better way to make certain that Julian Quist Associates loses all interest in Wally Best's plans?

The setting sun lighted the city's skyline as Quist drove across the George Washington Bridge and headed downtown to his office.

Gloria Chard, the receptionist, was still at her desk when Quist walked into the office—long after her usual quitting time. One look at her face told Quist that there was no good news waiting for him.

"Dan's in his office, Julian," she said.

"Thanks for standing by, Gloria," Quist said.

"You expected me to be somewhere else?" Gloria asked.

Garvey was talking on the phone to someone when Quist walked into his office. He looked up, scowling, saw who it was, and told his contact on the phone that he'd call back later.

"Nothing?" Quist asked.

Garvey shook his head. "The police won't officially consider someone missing till after twenty-four hours. But our old friend Sergeant Carter—Jake Carter—of Missing Persons has 'set things in motion,' whatever that means. He needs things that only you can help with. What she was wearing this morning when you last saw her. Assuming some message was fouled up, what friends might have asked her for help."

"She hadn't dressed when I left," Quist said. "She was wearing what I guess you call a housecoat."

"Is it still in the apartment? What clothes are missing from her wardrobe? Presumably she'd have dressed to come to the office. What's not there?"

"I'll recognize the housecoat if it's there," Quist said. "What she might have dressed in—Lydia has a shop full of clothes, you know."

"If she left under her own steam, she wouldn't have been dressed for a party," Garvey said.

"A party dress I might know," Quist said. "Skirts, blouses, sweaters—?" He shrugged. "What do you mean, 'left under her own steam'?"

"There are a lot of things that could have happened, Julian. She would have left for the office a few minutes before nine, all things being equal. Elevator in your building is automatic, so there was no man there. Busiest time of the day for the doorman. People leaving for work, wanting taxis. He doesn't remember seeing Lydia, but he could have been out at the curb trying to flag down a cab for someone. Nobody else has turned up to say they saw her, but that doesn't mean she wasn't there. So she starts to walk to the office as usual and is—intercepted."

"Or an accident?"

"If she was on the way to the office, her route was always the same. Sergeant Carter tells me there wasn't an accident reported in that area all day."

"So she passed out, fainted. Someone called an ambulance."

"Not on her route," Garvey said. "She could have been stopped, of course, a gun stuck in her ribs, herded into a waiting car."

"That suggests a careful plan," Quist said. "Someone who knew what her route would be—"

"If it wasn't a plan, we can feel a little better, a little more hopeful," Garvey said. "If it was planned, I have to believe it was planned in Bridgetown."

"If Lydia was attacked on her way to work, I hadn't even reached Bridgetown. If this was done to stop me—"

"You've been handling Wally for three or four days—press releases, TV interviews. Bridgetown has known for that long that you were involved. Plenty of time to plan."

"If so, then someone had to be missing from Bridgetown," Quist said.

"Why?" Garvey asked. "Everybody in Bridgetown could have an alibi. Manchester Arms could hire a terrorist from anywhere in the world—Libya, to Iran, to Nicaragua, or just some strong-arm guy here in New York. They have a network of operatives."

"So what do we do, just sit here and talk?" Quist asked.

"They haven't made any demands on you yet," Garvey said.

"Do they have to? I know what they want."

"So give it to them," Garvey said. "Drop Wally Best's campaign, wait, and pray that they'll turn Lydia loose when they're satisfied that you've quit."

"I could go back to Bridgetown, yank Mark Foreman out of his office, and throw him in the nearest incinerator if they don't hand Lydia over to me," Quist said, his voice shaking with anger.

"That way you'd be signing Lydia's death sentence," Garvey said.

Quist leaned forward, pressing the palms of his hands against his forehead.

"We have to make it appear that we are doing nothing," Garvey said.

" 'Appear'—?"

"We have to make it appear that we don't know Lydia is missing," Garvey said.

"But the whole office force—your policeman—the doorman at my apartment house—?"

"Message miscarried," Garvey said. "You knew all along that she was going off on a vacation, destination uncertain. Somehow you thought Lydia would inform us here at the office, she thought you would inform us. You go back to Bridgetown, handle the campaign there as though nothing's wrong. Spread the word that you were called back to New York because we thought something had happened to your lady. All a mistake. She's touring around the country somewhere."

"All they have to do is ask Lydia—if she's alive," Quist said. The last words almost strangled him.

"If she's alive," Garvey said, "she'll be smart enough to realize what's cooking and play it by ear, our way."

"You think she—?"

"She wants to live as badly as you want her to live," Garvey said.

How big a gamble do you take with a life that is more precious to you than your own? Dan Garvey tried to answer that question for Quist.

"These people in Bridgetown are killers, Julian," he said. "We know that. First there was Martha Best, then this Wilson girl, and now—Lydia."

"If she is dead, Dan—"

"If she's dead, Julian, I'll go with you to Bridgetown with an army of friends and we'll wipe those bastards off the face of the earth. I promise you that."

"Thanks. I—I—"

"But if she's alive, we have to play it very close to the vest."

"You think there's a chance?"

"I do, Julian. They want Wally out of their hair. If you drop out of the picture, they've got it made. If you don't, they have to have some way to bring pressure on you. If they can prove to you that Lydia is alive, by having her talk to you, you'll do whatever they demand—they think."

"And while we wait for that?"

"We have to sell them a fairy story."

"Like what?"

Garvey drew a deep breath. "I've been thinking. Lydia is a writer. My story goes like this: She's planning a novel. She's looking for a background, a small town somewhere in the southwest. She's been planning to go hunt for such a place, and today was the day. You knew she was going, but there was a mix-up. You thought she was going to notify us here at the office. She thought you were going to tell us. So, we sound an alarm. You come down here and straighten us out. You don't expect to hear from her until she finds a town where she'll stay for a week or so. You're not concerned, and when you explain this to us, we're not concerned."

"So?"

"So, you go back to Bridgetown to work for Wally."

"But if they know so much about us, they'll know it's not so," Quist said.

"They know a lot about us," Garvey said. "They know the route Lydia would take walking to work. They know you might bring Wally home a winner. But they don't know what your private conversations and plans are. No way. This story will explain why you're not concerned. They'll have to make a new move, and we'll be ready!"

"They'll never let Lydia go," Quist said. "She can describe who's got her."

"Who? A dark-skinned Arab with a black beard? That could be her description, which would get us and the police nowhere. Act out my story and you may have a day or two to sniff out something in Bridgetown. Sergeant Carter will be working for you here. Time—it's the only thing that can work for us."

You don't sleep on a decision that involves a life. People in the office were told what the "real story" was—Bobby Hilliard, Quist's "Jimmy Stewart" partner; Connie Parmalee, his secretary; Gloria, the receptionist; the switchboard girls. Connie was instructed to call the rest of the regular staff at their homes to let them know there was "nothing to worry about."

"You know I don't believe a word of this, Julian," Connie told him when they were alone in his office.

"If you give a hoot in hell about Lydia or me, you'd better act like you believe," Quist said. His voice had a grim sound to it that had never been there before when he spoke to Connie.

"I'll make believers of the whole world, if necessary," Connie said. She reached out to touch Quist's clenched fist, which was resting on his desk. "How bad is it, Julian?"

"Bad!" he said. "We may be able to buy a little time this way, the only time we'll ever have to find something we can use as a bargaining chip."

"What can I do?"

"I hoped you'd tell me what you could do," Quist said.

Connie nodded slowly. "People in the press, the media, we know. What's the gossip about Manchester Arms? Who are their undercover business partners? What's the dirt about individual big shots in the company, their love lives, the women they're not supposed to be keeping?"

"That's the very thing they're trying to stop," Quist said.

"But you're looking for it, not to save Lydia but to get Wally Best elected mayor of the town. As far as you know, Lydia is out somewhere researching the background for a novel. It's perfectly logical for you to be trying to gather ammunition for Wally to use in his campaign. They hold the ace card—Lydia. But they may not use it right away unless you do come up with something damaging. We have to hope and pray that that's the way it is."

"You're an angel!" Quist said. He pushed himself up from behind his desk. Fear for Lydia seemed to have turned his body into deadweight. "I'm headed back to Bridgetown, Connie. Don't call me at the hotel there. My phone calls will probably be monitored. I'm not sure our suite there isn't bugged. I'll call you on an outside phone when I get there, and every couple of hours after that. If you've got anything, if Dan's Sergeant Carter has come up with anything, report to me on my calls to you, not on any kind of calls to my room."

"You know that if Dan, Bobby, or I can do anything for you in Bridgetown, we'll be up there on the double."

"I know, luv," Quist said. "Right now, getting the goods on Manchester Arms and its people may be easier down here in New York than it will be in Bridgetown. They've got Bridgetown covered like a tent."

Connie nodded. "There are places to start down here."

"But it's always for information that will help Wally, remember. No mention of Lydia except that she's out somewhere doing research for a book. Anyone you talk to could be ready to report back to Mark Foreman and his crew in Bridgetown. There's no way of guessing who's been bought."

It was nearly midnight when Quist walked into the lobby of Bridgetown House, eyes red and tired from the long night drive. The very first people he saw were Captain Seaton and Luke Simmons, the baldheaded manager of the hotel. Simmons beckoned to Quist the minute he walked in the front entrance. "We heard you'd gone back to New York," he said.

"Wild-goose chase," Quist said. He looked at Seaton. "Anything new here?"

Seaton's eyes were narrowed, a cold glint in them. "Wild-goose chase?" he asked.

Quist laughed, trying to sound totally relaxed. "Had an emergency call from my office," he said. "A lady who's very important to me was missing, hadn't turned up at the office for work. It was a crazy foul-up. I knew she'd taken off on a research trip. I thought she'd notified the office; she obviously thought I had. My partners had actually had Missing Persons out looking for Lydia—Lydia Morton, my lady. I got it straightened out and came back. Two hundred miles of driving just to straighten out a stupid mistake. You seen my candidate anywhere?"

"Wally? He's up in your suite," Simmons said.

You can almost hear their brains ticking, Quist thought. They were telling themselves that Quist wouldn't be here, making jokes, if he didn't believe what he was telling them.

"Sleep is all I care about at the moment," Quist said. "See you around."

Wally was pacing restlessly around their living room when Quist let himself in, using the room key from the desk. He came forward, starting to speak. Quist made a quick silencing gesture, indicating again the possibility of a bug. Then he told Wally the story about Lydia's research trip. While he talked, laughing about the confusion in New York, he wrote the truth on a desk pad and handed it to Wally. When Wally had read it, Quist burned the paper in an ashtray. He went on talking about his trip, the confusion in New York, his exhaustion and need for sleep, said good night, and headed for his bedroom.

So far, so good.

The morning was a beautiful, sunny August day. Room service brought their ordered breakfast. Over coffee, Quist and Wally talked about the campaign. Their first stop that day would be at Maggie Nolan's to see if she had any plans for Wally to make personal appearances. It wasn't until they were in Quist's car, headed for Maggie Nolan's place at the top of the town, that Quist was able to give Wally the details about Lydia's disappearance. Wally looked to be in shock when he'd heard it all.

"You don't have to go on with this, Julian," he said in a shaken voice. "Back off, do what they want—anything to get Lydia free."

"I'm not staying with this for you, Wally," Quist said. "I'm staying with it because it may give Lydia her only chance."

"What can I do?"

Quist's laugh was short and sharp. "Get yourself elected," he said.

In Maggie Nolan's handsome front yard there was the sound of the clamor of dogs, but no sign of the lady. Quist wandered around toward the back of the house. There, a couple of dozen well-groomed dogs were clawing at the wire fence that penned them in. Maggie was there, feeding each dog a biscuit. The quality of the dogs' sounds changed, and Maggie turned and saw the two men.

"Hi!" she called out and came toward them. "I heard you'd gone back to New York, Julian."

"Where did you hear that?" Quist asked.

"Morning paper. Jerry Collins's boys don't miss much about the comings and goings of famous visitors. I read about it with my morning coffee."

"You tell anyone I was going?" Quist asked Wally.

"No!" Wally said. Then he shook his head. "Not exactly, that is. Simmons, the hotel manager, asked me. He said you'd gassed up your car and told the garage man you were headed for New York. He wanted to know if you were checking out. I told him I didn't think so."

"You tell him why I was going?"

"No. He didn't ask. He just wanted to know if you'd still be sharing the suite with me."

One way to find out if the word had gotten to him about Lydia, Quist thought. He told Maggie the invented story about Lydia and the alleged foul-up on messages.

"Must have thrown a scare into you until it got straightened out," Maggie said.

"Not really," Quist said. "Lydia is a lady who can take care of herself. You move at all for Wally?"

Maggie nodded. "Women's Rights, a local group, holds its regular monthly meeting this afternoon. I persuaded them to let Wally make his pitch to them." She smiled. "Sing them a song or two, of course. Come on into the house, and I'll tell you where and when and who you should butter up!"

While Maggie told Wally about places and people he'd be familiar with, Quist read the item in the *Journal.* It was in a column called "Up and Around," written by someone named Liz Davis.

Julian Quist, internationally known public relations expert, came to Bridgetown yesterday to help launch

Wally Best's campaign for mayor. Mr. Quist must have tested the climate here pretty thoroughly and discovered that Wally's juvenile attempt to become mayor of Bridgetown as an independent had about as much chance as the proverbial snowball in you-know-where. Mr. Quist returned to New York last night, obviously convinced. So much for impractical dreams.

They had been sure he wouldn't come back, sure that he'd stay quietly away from Bridgetown as long as he had any hopes for Lydia. Liz Davis, whoever she was, must have been given the story by Jerry Collins, the publisher of the *Journal*, and told how to handle it.

"It looks as if I go to the bathroom, they'll use it against Wally in some fashion," Quist said to Maggie as he handed the paper to Wally.

"All's fair in love and politics," Maggie said.

"So it seems."

"Liz Davis is popular here, read at every breakfast table," Maggie said. "But Jerry Collins does her political thinking for her."

"You know the lady?" Quist asked.

"Of course. She covers all the women's organizations here in town, and I belong to most of them."

"I think I'm going to ask her to retract this story in tomorrow's column," Quist said.

Maggie laughed. "Give Liz my love. I don't think you'll find her a pushover, Julian. She knows who feathers her nest."

Quist found himself under emotional pressures he'd never experienced before in his life. Just trying to appear as though he had no problems was almost more than he could manage. All around him, people had vital information that he didn't have. People like Captain Seaton, the homicide detective; Luke Simmons, the hotel manager; probably Jerry Collins, the *Journal*'s publisher and editor, and his lady columnist; certainly Mark Foreman, in his office at Manchester Arms, knew exactly where Lydia was, whether she was alive or dead, whether or not she had been injured in any way. They all knew exactly what he was going through, that his story of why he'd gone back to New York could not have a word of truth in it. They were just standing around, watching him squirm. The impulse to reach out, grab someone, and hammer the truth out of them was almost irresistible. But that could end any chance for Lydia. Right now they might hold off, trying to find out if there was any truth to Quist's "research" story about his lady. If there was, and he wasn't bluffing, they'd have to take a next step to let him know that Lydia was not working on the background for a novel. Would that be to let him hear her voice on the phone?

And Lydia. He had to tell himself over and over that she was alive and must be wondering what price was being asked for her release. Quist wondered, if he paid the price, which appeared to be a promise that he would back away from Wally, could they risk letting Lydia go? Or would she be held until after the election was over and Wally had lost—three months from now?

One other gnawing anxiety had to be faced. Maybe it had been a simple mugging on a city street, unconnected with Bridgetown or Manchester Arms. Maybe Lydia's body was in a back-alley trash can somewhere, or tossed into a city dump.

There was one risk he couldn't run. If he told Wally how greatly he feared for Lydia's safety, what would the young man's reaction be? Would he back off from his try at politics, or would his own deep wound break open and drive him out to do battle with an army he had no chance of defeating? Charges, without evidence to back them up, would destroy any chance to maneuver himself into a position where evidence might be found.

Finally, was there any way for Quist himself to find evidence that could be used as a bargaining chip to free Lydia? Local police were the enemy. State police would laugh at him unless he had something positive in hand. Bridgetown and Manchester Arms had everything going for them, and Quist had nothing going for him. He might have a few hours, a day or two, before they left him no alternatives about Lydia. It was difficult to realize that he must find some crucial evidence in the murder of Martha Best, and not devote himself to finding Lydia. Somewhere there was proof of some criminal activity involving Manchester Arms that Martha had found. She had been killed before she could use it. Whatever it was, it must still be there to be found, or else why try to force Quist off the trail by committing another crime? Was there any chance of finding what Martha had found before he was completely immobilized by the people who had Lydia? One in a million, Quist thought.

Quist persuaded Wally that he should circulate in the city, touch bases with all his old friends, prepare to charm Maggie Nolan's Women's Rights friends. While they were still at the top of the town, Quist decided he would try to throw a couple of curves at Liz Davis, the *Journal* columnist. A lady who was read over everyone's breakfast coffee in Bridgetown must be loaded with explosive dirt about people in her city.

Quist's reception at the *Journal* office was not what it had been when he'd had Wally with him. The receptionist was polite but not wide-eyed. She didn't think Miss Davis was available. She would inquire. When Quist gave his name, that seemed to light a small fire under her. She left her desk and was quickly back again.

"This way, Mr. Quist."

Liz Davis was in her own comfortably furnished small office. She was, Quist guessed, a woman in her early forties, dark-haired, brown eyes, rather more smartly dressed than you would expect in a small-town setting in the early morning. She was sitting behind a typewriter on a movable table, and she pushed a pair of horn-rimmed glasses up into her hair as Quist was brought in by the receptionist. Her smile, like so many other smiles in Bridgetown, was professional.

"So you've come back, Mr. Quist," she said.

"And read your column, Miss Davis," Quist said. "Which is why I'm here."

"Oh?"

"I think I need you to make a correction in tomorrow's column."

"Correction?"

"You're suggesting in today's column that I left Bridgetown last night because I'd discovered, in one day, that Wally Best doesn't have a chance in Bridgetown's political arena."

"And you've changed your mind and think he has?"

"I haven't changed my mind, because I've never thought he didn't have a chance," Quist said. "My trip to New York had nothing to do with Wally at all." He sketched out the story of Lydia's "research trip" and the supposed foul-up in messages at his New York office.

Liz Davis listened, taking the glasses down out of her hair and putting them on the table beside her typewriter.

"When we learned a few days ago that Julian Quist Associates was going to handle Wally's campaign, I did some research on you and your company, Mr. Quist. I learned about your relationship with Lydia Morton, which is no secret in your world. You must have had a bad time when you were told she was missing."

"Not really," Quist said. "I knew there had to be some kind of screw-up. Lydia isn't the kind of person who can be easily tricked into trouble."

"But you haven't heard from her?"

"Nor expect to for a day or two. When she finds a place to light, she'll let me know. My problem is with you, Miss Davis. I take it for granted that you and I will be on opposite sides of the fence in this mayoral campaign. Your boss, Jerry Collins, has made it quite clear that the *Journal* will be supporting Greg Martin. But it seems to me that an invention like yours, that I left town because I found Wally's cause hopeless, is a foul ball. I think I'm entitled to a statement from you that you misread the situation."

She reached forward, picked up her glasses, and fiddled with them. He could almost read her mind. How much pressure could he bring to bear on her?

"I suppose your friends on national television and radio will be willing to make a big deal out of it," she said.

" 'What's sauce for the goose . . . ,' " Quist said. "We can play this thing on the level, or we can see who can throw the biggest rocks."

Her smile was thin and tight, not the professional charmer. "So you're declaring war, Mr. Quist?"

"Sure it's a war," he said. "A political war. But if you lie about me, I'll have to fight back with whatever I have."

"And what do you have?"

"I haven't researched you yet, Miss Davis, as you say you have researched me. But I can have an army of skilled professionals working on it in about a half an hour."

The stems of her glasses made a ticking noise as she tapped them against the typewriter. "Can I tell your story about why you really went to New York?" she asked.

"Sure. It's no secret," Quist said. "But I think you should add that I'm a long way from giving up on Wally."

"Fair enough," the lady said. "Read 'Up and Around' tomorrow morning."

Quist gave her his most ingratiating smile. It hid his real thought, which was a question whether this woman knew where Lydia really was. "Can we talk about things in general?"

"For not too long, Mr. Quist. I've got to plan that new column for tomorrow."

"So, what could be lost if Wally Best managed to get elected mayor?" Quist asked. "Manchester Arms would still control the city's economy, supply a majority of jobs, have too many people indebted to them, grateful to them, to lose any control of the local machinery. Actually Wally, popular all around the country, even around the world, could be an asset to them. Support him and they could become good guys to millions of people—and lose nothing."

"Have you suggested that to Mark Foreman?"

"I hinted at it in our only meeting. He'll be hearing it over radio and television for the next couple of months. Maybe if he hears it often enough—"

Liz Davis laughed. "Mark Foreman doesn't take naturally to heat," she said.

"He is the key man in the Manchester Arms powerhouse?" Quist asked.

Liz Davis hesitated, as though she needed to think about her answer. She must have been an extremely pretty young girl, Quist thought. Right now she had that endearing look that the very young acquire when they're trying to concentrate on a puzzle.

"I guess Foreman is the 'key man,' " she said, "but he's only one member of what I guess you'd call an 'inner circle.' Men like Seymour Sloan, Greg Martin, and others. I think that inner circle dictates the policies, the strategics of Manchester Arms. Foreman has been put out in front, the spokesman, the apparent boss. But I think that inner circle can say 'No' to him."

Quist found himself intrigued. Liz Davis didn't sound like someone on the inside, but she probably was, he told himself. That he was only one of a group, an "inner circle," may have been exactly what Mark Foreman wanted the outside world to think, and the lady was conveying his message.

"Your column tomorrow will have to comment on the murder of Sue Wilson," Quist said.

"Which is why I have to leave you presently to dig out what facts I can about it. I can begin with you, Mr. Quist. What would a thief have been looking for in your room and Wally Best's?"

Quist tried a casual shrug. "Wally is famous and rich," he said. "I'm not exactly infamous and poor. A hotel thief could assume we might have something worth taking."

"Early reports make it sound as though he was looking for something specific," Liz Davis said.

"Big things come in small packages," Quist said. "It has occurred to me that someone thought we might have some special ammunition to use in Wally's campaign."

"What kind of special ammunition?"

"Somewhere in this town, Miss Davis, is the murderer of Martha Best. That crime isn't going to be forgotten during the campaign, can't be forgotten. Do Wally or I, his agent, have any kind of evidence pointing to Martha's killer?"

"Oh, wow!" the woman said. "You really think that?"

"As I said, I thought of it as a motive," Quist said. "But since we don't have any evidence of that kind, it's just a wild guess. But I need to be ready for questions about Martha when we get really going. You must have covered her story in your column. I'd like to know what you thought about it at the time. I suppose I can find back files of the *Journal* in the public library. But if you wanted to be friendly, you undoubtedly have copies of your columns right here."

"I have no reason to make it difficult for you," Liz Davis said. She turned her swivel chair toward her desk and opened a drawer. "When I heard you and Wally were coming to town, I went back into the files myself and took out the columns on Martha Best to refresh my memory. It was almost six months ago, you know." She took a manila envelope out of the drawer and handed it to Quist. "While you look at these, I'd like to go out to the newsroom and see if there's anything new on the Wilson case."

A cooperative enemy, Quist thought as he watched her go. Still, there'd be nothing here that he wouldn't have found at the public library.

"Up and Around," the woman's column, was often witty, revealed a shrewd observer, and was certainly not a medium for unverified gossip. Liz Davis was a first-rate reporter and commentator. Quist was a qualified judge of this kind of work, and Liz Davis, he told himself, was first class.

When she came back, reporting that there was nothing new on Sue Wilson except that she was officially dead, she added that the district attorney was calling it Murder One.

"I'm impressed," Quist said, pointing to the stack of columns on the desk beside him.

Liz smiled. " 'Praise from Caesar—' " she said.

"But you left out some of it," Quist said. "Martha disappeared on a Wednesday night. Your first mention of it doesn't appear until the following Monday. She was Mark Foreman's secretary. That would make her news in Bridgetown, but you didn't comment for five days on the fact that she was missing." He handed the columns back to her, but she didn't even glance at them.

"Martha Best disappeared the night of the blizzard," she said. "That was a Wednesday. My Thursday column was already written and set up in type. Thursday there were a thousand stories about the storm, people trapped, kids lost on their way home, traffic accidents. It wasn't until late that day that Mark Foreman let it be known that Martha hadn't turned up for work. Friday's column was already in the hopper. 'Up and Around' doesn't appear on Saturdays and Sundays. So my first mention of Martha didn't appear until Monday. Her being missing might not have been worth space in my column if Wally hadn't shown up in town on Friday and offered a reward to anyone who could find her. Wally is news wherever he goes. Also he came to me, asking for help—through my column. So my first mention of Martha came that Monday." She tapped the pile of columns. "I simply wrote that she hadn't turned up after the storm and that Wally was in town, offering a reward to anyone who could locate his sister. I still didn't think it was anything but one of the freak aftermaths of the storm. People didn't get messages; friends and families were separated, stayed in different places that first couple of nights. Martha lived alone, didn't have any family here in town. She didn't have any reason to explain her absence to anyone but Mark Foreman, her boss. I was sure she'd turn up on Monday for work with a perfectly good explanation. Of course, she didn't."

"But you kept mentioning her each day after that."

Liz shrugged. "Two reasons. Mark Foreman also asked for my help. Local radio stations and national TV were making a big thing of it. And Wally—he had me nervous."

"How?"

"He told me Martha had had something on Manchester Arms and was about to spill it. Manchester *is* this town, my town. I didn't believe Martha could have anything on the company that everybody didn't know. Big industry deals with anyone who will buy, friend or enemy. It wouldn't have shocked anyone to hear that Manchester Arms was selling weapons to terrorists who used those weapons against Americans. The world of big business is a cynical world. But she might have had something on one man, one officer of the company. Mark Foreman, her boss, would have to be my first choice."

"You didn't suggest that in any of your columns?"

"I'm a reporter, not a speculator," Liz said.

Quist smiled. "And if you had mentioned the idea that Mark Foreman is the villain in Martha Best's murder, your boss, Jerry Collins, would have fired you before you could turn around."

"If I had had facts, I'd have run that risk," Liz said.

"Yet Martha's killer has to be local," Quist said. "He didn't disappear in the blizzard. He was here several days later to move Martha's body. He was here months later to search Wally Best's room and mine, and to murder Sue Wilson. He's here in Bridgetown, walking around free as a bird, while Seaton, the homicide dick, and the rest of the powers-that-be sit around whistling Dixie."

"Needle-in-a-haystack department," Liz said. "You just fumble around until your finger gets pricked. Somebody will come up with something one of these days. It could even be me."

"You're saying that you're looking?"

"Can I pretend, after what happened to Sue Wilson in your room, Mr. Quist, that there isn't a story out there? Question for you, and then I have to get to work. Do you think Wally is in any danger if he insists on running?"

"If it looks as if he can win, who knows?" Quist said.

"At least you've got time before there'll be any indications of a winner, one way or the other." Liz stood up. It was a signal that the interview was over. "Let me know when you hear where your Lydia decides to research her novel. I'll be fascinated. If you hear from her—"

Quist froze in the doorway. "Just what is that supposed to mean?"

"My dear Julian, do you think any intelligent person giving this whole situation any thought at all can buy your story about Lydia Morton? A mixed-up or missed message you could have settled in two minutes on the phone. Instead you race off to New York to set up a fake story."

Quist felt an icy chill running down his spine. "I should have guessed where you stand," he said.

"One last word, Mr. Quist," Liz said. "I am my own person. I'm not a spy for anyone. Believe whatever you choose, but that's the way it is. If I can be useful, you're welcome to come back."

Chapter Two

The morning was slipping away without anything being accomplished. If Liz Davis was what common sense told Quist she had to be, a spy for the inner circle at Manchester Arms, then, shortly after she reported on her interview with him, he could expect some kind of threatening demand with Lydia's safety at stake if he refused to follow orders.

One question began to gnaw at Quist. Liz Davis had pointed out that the election was almost three months away. It would be a couple of months before polls would show whether Wally had any chance at all against Greg Martin, Manchester's candidate. The question was, why violence so early? Why the kidnapping of Lydia at this stage of the game? It had happened some time before the search of his room and Wally's and the murder of Sue Wilson. That sequence of horrors suggested that Wally and Quist were on the verge of discovering something fatal to Greg Martin's chances. If they were, Quist told himself with some bitterness, they had no notion of it themselves. Lydia was the trump card to be used against them if they stumbled onto a secret that had already cost Martha Best her life and Sue Wilson hers when she accidentally walked in on someone searching Quist's room. That search suggested that someone thought Quist and Wally might already have possession of the secret.

Going back over what they knew, it was fairly obvious that Martha Best's apartment had been carefully searched before anyone even knew that she was missing. No notes, no letters, no documents in her apartment, according to Captain Seaton. True or false? Had there been something there that Seaton had removed? That would have been an early guess before Lydia had been abducted and Sue Wilson murdered. Now it seemed that whatever was dangerous to someone hadn't been found, and the enemy had to be sure that if Quist and Wally found it before they did, they wouldn't use it—to save Lydia.

Quist found a pleasant surprise waiting for him when he got back to Bridgetown House. Dan Garvey was sitting in a leather armchair near the front entrance. Quist's first question was whether there'd been any news about Lydia.

"Nothing," Garvey said. "And my friend Sergeant Carter hasn't come up with anything either. The action has to be here in Bridgetown, and I hoped I might be useful."

Quist explained that a conversation in his suite might not be safe, and he and Dan walked down the street to a bar and grill. It was still early for the lunch crowd, and the two friends got a corner table to themselves, ordered coffee and sandwiches, and waited to be free of the waiter. When they'd been served, Quist brought Dan up to date, most particularly his interview with Liz Davis.

"No matter where you turn, you find someone who's a pipeline to Foreman and his friends," Dan said.

"They think we're onto something," Quist said. "I wish to God we were."

"But if you were, you couldn't use it."

"Lydia?"

Garvey nodded. "Something was nagging at me while I was driving up here," he said. "I only saw Martha Best once or twice when we were launching Wally some ten years ago. I suppose she was about twenty then, sensational looking, with the kind of energy that would light up the sky. A sexy, exciting gal."

"I agree. So?"

"In the last six months, since she was killed, I haven't heard a word about a boyfriend, or boyfriends. There had to be a man or men in her life. You'd think they'd have come forward, offering to help. I never heard of one who did. Wally ever mention a guy in her life?"

Quist shook his head slowly, trying to remember. "I don't think he ever mentioned anyone, nor has the subject ever come up in our conversations. Point was made at the time that Martha lived alone, so there was no one there she might have called the night of the blizzard."

"She wouldn't have become a nun at thirty," Garvey said.

"When I talked to Mark Foreman, he mentioned how attractive she was, physically," Quist said. "Said he made a pass at her and got a 'No,' but didn't think he'd gotten a 'Never.' "

"Attractive gal, sister of a famous man. Difficult to hide her sex life from an inquisitive world."

"You're suggesting that if we could locate the guy, he might help to get us on the track of the motive for killing Martha?"

"If he could do that, why hasn't he done it before now?" Garvey asked.

"I can think of one reason," Quist said. "He's married."

"And I can think of another," Garvey said. "He works for Manchester Arms. He's someone Martha met when she went to work there."

"So he killed his lover to keep her from blowing up his world?"

"Could be," Garvey said. "Let's see if Wally can fill us in."

"Why wouldn't he have come forward before this?"

"Who knows?" Garvey said. "His sister is having an affair with a married man. Wally has no reason to suspect or distrust that man, and so there is no reason to publicize an illicit love affair."

"That could be it, I suppose," Garvey said.

"So let's find Wally and put it to him." Garvey finished the last of his coffee. "In a strange way, it could fit, you know? They searched Martha's apartment after she was dead, looking for letters from her lover? So, they found some or they didn't, eliminating any traces of him in the apartment. Six months later they search Wally's room and yours. Maybe Martha mentioned her lover in a letter to her brother. She might also have mentioned his name to you somewhere along the way, or Wally could have told you and you'd made some kind of a record of it for use in the campaign. Let's get to Wally. At least we might come up with a name."

The Women's Rights meeting was being held at the Bridgetown Country Club, not far from Maggie Nolan's place at the top of the hill. There was another beautiful view down toward the river, overlooking a rolling golf course. There were a handful of players in sight, but there must have been more than a hundred cars parked around the clubhouse. Women's Rights had turned out in force, it seemed.

Inside the clubhouse, Quist and Garvey were stopped by a uniformed attendant.

"I'm sorry, but this is a private party," the man said.

"I know," Quist said. "But Wally Best is our client. I think we're entitled."

"Let me check," the man said. He crossed to a door and opened it. From inside came the sound of many female voices all talking at once. The man came back with a good-looking woman with dark red hair and that perpetual professional smile that Quist had come to expect in Bridgetown.

"You're Mr. Quist, aren't you?" the woman said to Garvey.

"I'm Dan Garvey, his partner," Dan said. "This is Julian Quist."

The woman turned to Quist. "It's a pleasure to meet you, Mr. Quist. I seem to have been appointed the doorwoman for the club. My name is Nancy Martin. Of course you may come in. The fireworks are about to be set off."

It was a kind of ballroom with a stage at the far end. Folding chairs had been set up, and they were all occupied by chattering females. But on the stage were men. Wally was one of them, but the others came as a surprise to Quist. He saw Mark Foreman; Greg Martin, who was running against Wally; Seymour Sloan, the chairman of Manchester Arms' board of directors; Bart Havens, the shaven-headed security chief for Manchester; and one or two others whom he didn't recognize.

"My husband is about to open the show," the redheaded woman said.

Nancy Martin! Could she be Greg Martin's wife?

Maggie Nolan came out of the crowd. "This isn't exactly what I thought it would be," she said to Quist. He introduced her to Dan. "I thought it would be just Wally, but the Manchester crowd wanted to speak their piece, too, and the ladies decided to let them."

"The two men on the left?" Quist asked.

"Jay Thompson and Ted Devens, both members of Manchester's board of directors," Maggie said. "They've brought out all their big guns. I'm glad you're here, Julian. Wally may need help."

A white-haired woman had stepped to the front of the stage and held up her hands for silence.

"Betty Lewis," Maggie whispered to Quist as the room was suddenly quiet. "She's president of Women's Rights."

"As most of you know," Betty Lewis said, "this meeting was planned for us to meet Wally Best and get acquainted with him." Interrupted by applause, she held up her hands again for quiet. "But Greg Martin, who is running on the Republican ticket, offered to come so that we could meet both candidates at the same time and give them each a chance to tell us where they stand." She turned and gestured toward the gray-haired

Martin, looking handsome in his Brooks Brothers summer suit. "Most of you don't need an introduction to Greg."

There was another round of applause, if anything a little louder than the handclapping for Wally.

Betty Lewis smiled. "We tossed a coin to determine who would speak first, and it gives me pleasure to ask Greg Martin to address you."

As Martin came forward, Quist identified the men on the platform for Garvey.

"Our boy's going to be snowed under," Garvey said. "That coin they tossed must have had two heads on it."

Martin had the poise of an experienced speaker. His smile was intimate, but not too intimate. He was talking to friends—even if he didn't know them.

"Maybe I got lucky on that coin toss," he said. "If Wally had gotten the chance to sing for you first, I might never have gotten out here at all." The women enjoyed the joke, and he was underway. "There are almost three months ahead for Wally and me; debating issues, picking popular causes to back. But Wally has the edge on me in one area. I hoped that I could use this occasion to make it clear to him—and to everyone else in Bridgetown—that this is one area in which I am with Wally one hundred percent." Martin's smile disappeared. "Six months ago a terrible tragedy struck this city. A beautiful, vital, important girl—'woman,' I suppose, in chronological terms—was brutally murdered. She was Martha Best, Wally's sister."

A murmur of sympathy moved across the audience.

"Good-looking and smart, too," Garvey muttered.

Martin went on. "There's a question that some of us have been asking ourselves for the last week or so, since Wally announced that he was running for mayor. Why would a young man who is already rich, famous, and popular all around the world want to be mayor of a small manufacturing city? We heard the talk—that he grew up here, that it was a childhood dream, and finally that it would be a way to honor his sister's memory. I have never really believed those explanations."

Martin turned to look at Wally, who was sitting, suddenly rigid, just off to his left. "I don't mean to say that I don't believe Wally may think those are his reasons. But much deeper down, he must be thinking that if he could get into a position of power here in Bridgetown, he might be able to solve a problem that none of the rest of us have been able to—name the murderer of his sister."

Another murmur ran through the audience of women.

"There's nothing wrong, God knows, about that being his goal. If I were in his shoes, that would be all I'd dream and think about, night and day. It's not only normal for him to feel that way, he should be applauded for it."

The murmur of voices swelled a little.

"There has been ugly talk in the last six months," Martin went on. "Martha Best worked for Mark Foreman, the top official in Manchester Arms." He gestured toward Foreman, who sat, quietly, at the far right on the stage. He wasn't an unattractive man, Quist thought, out of his work clothes, wearing a light tan summer tweed jacket. "The talk has been that Martha, in her confidential position, had access to business dealings that Manchester might not want to have made public. In short, that she was killed to keep her from exposing those secrets."

The audience's voices became an excited chatter. Martin had to hold up his hands for quiet.

"He's unloading Wally's gun," Garvey said to Quist.

"Let me tell you," Martin went on when the room had quieted. "I don't believe for an instant that that's true. I have been involved with Manchester ever since I was a water boy in one of the boiler rooms. I've known the men who're sitting here on the platform most of my adult life: Mark Foreman, Seymour Sloan, Jay Thompson, Ted Devens, Bart Havens. It's impossible for me to imagine that any of them could be involved in the crime of murder. I would take my oath that Manchester Arms has nothing to hide. A big corporation like ours, doing business with a world market, may have dealings that sometimes puzzle the unsophisticated. But murder to cover them? Never.

Don't misunderstand, I'm not here to defend Manchester Arms against an accusation that hasn't actually been made. I'm here to discuss a campaign for mayor with Wally and me as leading candidates. If Wally wants to be mayor so that he will be in a better position to come on the truth about his sister, I'm here to offer him a way out. He doesn't have to be mayor of Bridgetown to have complete access to the files and records of Manchester Arms." Martin turned toward Mark Foreman.

Manchester's president nodded and spoke without rising. "Wally can see anything he wants to see. His friend Julian Quist, whom I see in the audience, can have the same freedom. Any special investigator Wally wants to hire will be just as free."

Martin turned to Bart Havens, the Telly Savalas–type security chief. Havens grinned. "Wally can see all the records of our investigation, and I'll assign a couple of men to help him, if he wants."

A loud round of applause from the audience.

Martin turned to Seymour Sloan, who rose to speak.

"As most of you know, Mayor Marple is too ill to be present at this meeting. But he's assured me that the city police, including Captain Seaton, who is still in charge of the case, will give Wally complete cooperation, supply him with any information they have."

The applause was noisy. Martin turned to Wally, smiling. "So there you are, Wally. If your reason for running is that you want to be in a position to get information that hasn't been available to you up to now, the town is yours, the records are yours, and you don't need to be mayor to get what you need. You've had public promises here from everyone who has the power to fulfill them. You won't have to back away from your career, the public that loves you as a singer and performer. Politics isn't your game, boy, and we've promised you, in public, to provide you with everything you could get if you were elected. Come down here, Wally, and tell us what you think."

Loud, loud applause as Wally came slowly, rather uncertainly, to stand beside Martin. Martin's signal for silence quieted the audience. Everyone in the place was focused on Wally. Quist's voice, loud and clear, came from the rear of the hall.

"I'd like to speak for my client if he'll let me!"

"Mr. Julian Quist, Wally's agent," Martin told the audience.

Quist walked forward to the speakers' platform. "I would like to offer Wally some advice before he makes a decision," he said. "Mr. Martin is right, of course, when he says that solving his sister's murder can never be out of Wally's mind. Anything else would be abnormal. But I'm quite convinced that solving that vicious murder is not the basic reason Wally is running for office. Long ago, when he and Martha were children, they dreamed that someday Wally would run for mayor and become the top man in town. The dream hasn't quite come true in all details. Wally isn't running against Mayor Marple, but against the mayor's would-be successor, Greg Martin. Making that dream come true is more important than ever now to Wally. Martha had shared it with him, and now that she's gone, Wally would like to make it come true in her memory."

A murmur of sympathy rose in the audience.

Quist proceeded. "Sentimental and romantic dreams rarely come true, but I could also say 'never come true' if you don't work for them. Wally would like to be the best mayor Bridgetown has ever had. A man who is trying for that, despite his lack of political experience, might turn out to be a miracle man if the people were to choose him."

Applause, applause.

"Naturally, along the way, Wally will keep his eyes wide open for any clue to his sister's murder, and I'm sure he will be enormously grateful for the help this group on the platform has offered him. But that offer of help is no reason for Wally to back away from a dream." Quist looked directly at Wally. "The decision is, of course, his."

Wally came down to the front of the stage, almost uncertainly. He looked out over the audience of women as if he were asking them to help him decide. The result was a spontaneous outbreak.

"Dream your dream, Wally!"

"Run for mayor!"

"Sing for us, Wally!"

"Sing, sing, sing!"

From somewhere backstage a young girl appeared carrying a guitar. She handed it to Wally. Slowly, a smile lit up his face, and he struck a chord or two on the instrument. The shouting subsided, and he began with the song that had launched him to stardom.

I'm a Rat Pack bad guy
But I'm the one who loves you.
I'm a Rat Pack hoodlum
But I'm the guy who loves you.

Many of the women knew the lyrics to the song and began to join in with him after the first few lines.

"Pretty hard to beat," a male voice said at Quist's elbow. Quist turned and found himself facing a smiling Greg Martin.

"That one sold over a million records," Quist said.

"I can only hope they'll get tired of it during the next three months," Martin said.

"He's got others," Quist said.

Martin laughed. "They all sound alike to me. You care to give me some free advice, Quist?"

"Try me," Quist said.

Still chuckling, Martin asked: "How do I make myself lovable?"

"You already have," Quist said. "Offering to help Wally solve his sister's murder was lovable in spades."

"I hope so," Martin said, his smile fading. "I wish there was something, somewhere, that would help clean that slate."

"So do I," Quist said, looking straight at Martin. "However, my job is to help make a dream come true."

They stood silent for a moment, listening to the caterwauling of the women.

"What chance do cold, hard facts have against that kind of sentimental love affair?" Martin asked, gesturing toward the Women's Rights crowd.

"Make the cold, hard facts come out sounding like 'mother,' " Quist said.

It was almost twilight before Quist, Garvey, and Wally were able to break away from the women at the country club. Wally was flexing his right hand as they got into Quist's car in the parking lot.

"You get writer's cramp after signing four or five hundred autographs?" he asked.

"More autographs than people," Garvey said.

"There's always a kid or another relative at home who wants one, too," Wally said.

"Seems like you could prepare something in advance that you could hand out," Garvey said.

"They want you to sign it 'for me,' " Wally said.

"I think we should go somewhere we can talk," Quist said as he started the car.

"The great outdoors sounds the best to me," Garvey said. "They can't bug the open countryside."

They found a place near the top of the town, looking down over the city and out to the river, where the late sunshine painted streaks of flame on the calm surface. Quist and Wally, in the front seats, turned around to face Garvey, who was behind them.

"I was all ready to throw in the towel on the election after Martin's speech," Wally said. "Then you came along, Julian—"

Garvey laughed. "It's not a too well-known fact, but Julian wrote Lincoln's Gettysburg Address for him."

"They expected you to back off, Wally," Quist said.

"Why would they care?" Wally asked. "They don't think I can win."

"They may not be sleeping too well tonight," Garvey said. "The kind of thing that happened there with those dames can snowball."

"I think the most important thing that happened up there is that they told us that there is nothing to be found in the files or records of Manchester Arms, or in the city records or police records, that will lead us to Martha's killer."

"They've had six months to get rid of anything that might be incriminating," Garvey said.

"But they searched our rooms," Wally said. "Killed Sue Wilson when she walked in on them."

"Last bit of insurance before they opened up the records to you," Quist said. "Somebody knew that Martha was out to get them, to 'make the headlines,' as she told you, Wally. They had to be certain she hadn't turned something over to you, and you to me. Sue Wilson nearly fouled it up for them."

"I'd like to make you both a bet," Garvey said. "I'd like to bet you, Julian, that you and Wally would never have found rooms anywhere else in town except in Bridgetown House. Now there's all this talk about how somebody got the passkey to your rooms. I'd like to bet you that ever since those locks were installed on the seventh floor at Bridgetown House, a passkey has been in the hands of someone at Manchester Arms."

"Why?" Wally asked.

"A place to accommodate business guests, business rivals, political opponents—like you, Wally. You steer the sucker to one of the rooms on that seventh floor—" Garvey shrugged.

"Nobody steered us!" Wally said.

"You walked into it like babes in the woods," Garvey said. "You chose Bridgetown House on your own. But your names were on a 'watch for' list, and you were promptly assigned rooms to which they had access without any problems. When they had to move you, you can bet your last buck they have the same kind of access to the suite you're in, plus a monitored phone and probably a bug planted somewhere."

"Well organized," Quist said.

"I know the type," Garvey said. "They don't leave anything to chance." He shifted his attention to Wally. "I was asking Julian a question when you started to 'Rat Pack Lover' those ladies out of their skulls. I've never heard anyone mention a boyfriend for your sister. As far as I know, no one in the last six months has claimed to be or to have been Martha's guy. The closest thing to romance came from Mark Foreman. She said 'No' but maybe not 'Never.' "

Wally sat, frowning thoughtfully, for a moment. "Martha was a very private kind of person."

"But close to you," Garvey said. "What was she—thirty years old when she died?"

"Thirty-one," Wally said.

"So you grew up together. You must have known who she dated."

Wally nodded, a faint smile moving his lips. "In seventh grade, yes. There was a kid named Johnny Tobias. He was off his rocker about Martha."

"Let's age her a little," Garvey said.

"So high school. There was a herd of them. She was a knockout, you know."

"I know," Garvey said. "Which is why I keep asking myself why nobody's come forward to say that a piece of that knockout girl was his. Surely she must have confided in you."

"To tell you the truth, she didn't," Wally said. "You know what the last ten years of my life have been like. Concerts, records, all away from here. I was lucky if I saw Martha once every six months. Martha was here, going to business school, graduating and getting a job with a subsidiary company of Manchester Arms across the river in Poughkeepsie. Then she got a call to fill in for Mark Foreman's secretary, who was killed in a car accident. She stayed with that job until she died."

"After telling you she was going to make headlines by revealing some scandal about Manchester Arms," Quist said.

"Let's not get away from the boyfriend," Garvey said.

Wally shrugged. "I asked her a couple of times, and she just laughed and said, 'You go to your church, and I'll go to mine.' "

"A woman as attractive as Martha doesn't go to her church alone," Garvey said.

"Which suggests something to me," Quist said. "There must be a hundred attractive young men working at Manchester Arms. There's the adage about not mixing business with pleasure. Which suggests Martha's guy was someone who worked for Manchester. They didn't want to go public with it, subject themselves to office gossip, office jokes."

"But someone working at Manchester has to know. You can't keep something like that hidden for four years!" Garvey said. "Who else did she date? A girl as attractive as Martha can't go dateless without attracting as much curiosity as open dating would cause. What's the talk? Who was guessing what about her? You must know people who work at Manchester, Wally."

"Not in Martha's part of it," Wally said after a moment. "My old friends, the Rat Pack gang, haven't gotten any higher up than working in the company garage, or driving a car for one of the big shots."

"Your friend Bobby Shanks?" Quist asked.

"Bobby drives a trash truck for them," Wally said.

"But he hears gossip," Quist said, "especially about the sister of a close friend."

"I suppose so," Wally said. "But I don't understand why this is so important."

"Because if Martha was having a thing with someone in the company, she'd have shared secrets with him," Garvey said. "She told you she was going to make headlines by blowing the lid off Manchester Arms. She'd tell her boyfriend what she had, wouldn't she?"

"So why hasn't he come forward?" Wally asked.

"Because he doesn't want to get on their hit list, too," Garvey said.

"Maybe Bobby Shanks should be our next stop," Quist said.

"His work day is probably over by now," Wally said. "We'd probably find him at the Pack Trap. That's a bar run by Martha's grammar school boyfriend, Johnny Tobias. It's a joint where most of the pack from my time hang out, and the new kids of today's pack."

"Show us the way," Garvey said.

"One question first," Wally said, focusing on Quist. "I expected you to back off because of Lydia. Can you risk going ahead with things?"

Quist's face turned stony. "How long I don't know, Wally," he said. "I've had no demands, no threats. I think they believe I believe Lydia has gone on a research trip. Until I get in their way, they're letting it ride, knowing they can stop me in my tracks if they have to. They're not worried about the election—yet. As long as I don't get onto something in the process that will be dangerous to them . . ." He left it there.

"Let's find Mr. Shanks," Garvey said.

The Pack Trap was a "joint" in the slang meaning of the word. There was a bar, a few scattered tables, a jukebox running full blast. The walls were decorated with pictures of nude ladies cut from *Playboy* and other magazines. The customers were three-to-one young males.

A shout went up as someone recognized Wally as he walked in with Quist and Garvey. Wally was quickly surrounded, backslapped. Word had already reached here, it seemed, about his success at the Women's Rights meeting. Bobby Shanks emerged from the crowd and came over to Quist and Garvey, who were standing to one side.

"Hear you just had a big success," Bobby said.

Quist introduced Garvey.

"Oh, boy!" Bobby said. "You gave me some of the biggest thrills in my life, Dan. Remember that championship game with the Bears? You ran for two touchdowns in that game. Made me rich! I had a five-dollar bet on your guys. Big money in those days."

"Not a game I'll ever forget," Garvey said.

"I should think not. If you're working for Wally, you'll get him an awful lot of male votes in this town. He's got a real chance, doesn't he, Julian?"

First names before you've taken a step, Quist thought.

"Come over to the bar," Bobby said. "Drinks on the house."

A younger man with an amiable smile served them. He was introduced as Johnny Tobias.

"You used to be one of Martha Best's boyfriends, didn't you, Johnny?" Garvey asked.

"Long ago," Tobias said. "Seventh grade."

"Johnny's married now, four kids," Bobby Shanks said. "He and Martha are ancient history."

They moved away to a table a few feet from the end of the bar. A nude lady smiled down at them from the wall.

"One of the things that's been interesting us, Bobby," Garvey said, sipping his beer, "is who Martha's boyfriend was at the time she was killed. He's never come forward."

Bobby Shanks grinned. "You aren't the only one wondering," he said. "I been wondering for several years."

"A guess?" Garvey asked.

"A lot of us who 'knew her when' have been guessing," Bobby said. "When she first came back here about four years ago to work for Mark Foreman, a few of us who'd known her earlier tried dating her. I brought her here, took her to a few movies, stuff like that. I wasn't the only one. But after about a month she backed away. No more dates."

"Who was she seen with?"

"Would you believe that in all that time, for more than three years before she died, I never saw her with anyone? I asked around—who was she going with? No one seemed to know. No one had seen her with anyone. We figured she had some guy out of town, Poughkeepsie or some place else she'd worked."

"But he never showed up here?"

"Not that I know of, or any of my friends know of."

"It couldn't be someone working at Manchester Arms?" Quist asked.

"Why hide it?" Bobby asked. "Unless—"

"Unless what?"

"Unless it's a big shot in the company who's married and has to keep it a secret," Bobby said.

"Her boss, Mark Foreman?"

"He's not married," Bobby said. "He's never made a secret about chasing after the attractive girls who work for Manchester."

"Someone else?"

"I can only tell you that whoever it was, he and Martha kept it swept clear under the rug."

"An affair kept that secret must have been very important to Martha," Quist said.

"And the secrecy very important to the man," Garvey said. "Martha had no reason to keep a romance a secret."

"Like I said, the guy was probably married," Bobby Shanks said.

"Playing out a romance in secret for more than three years suggests Martha must have been very much in love," Quist said.

Bobby Shanks grinned. "Yeah, like in the movies. Guy's wife is hopelessly sick, he has kids he has to keep from knowing. Robert Redford and Meryl Streep."

"Did Martha have some close woman friend?" Quist asked. "She might have confided in another woman."

"No one in our world I can think of," Bobby Shanks said. "But she was real good friends with that doll who writes a column for the *Journal*."

"Liz Davis?" Quist was surprised.

"I saw them lunching at several different places," Shanks said. "Martha liked the big shots. That's why I'm guessing the guy was someone high up in Manchester Arms."

"The Davis woman mention to you that she and Martha were friends?" Garvey asked Quist.

Quist shook his head. "I didn't ask. She didn't volunteer anything."

"She might have answers to the whole puzzle."

"Then why has she kept it out of print?" Quist asked.

"Told to her in confidence by a friend," Garvey suggested. "If you dropped it in her lap, she might be willing to tell you something."

"It's worth a try," Quist said.

It was early evening when Quist called the *Journal* and asked for Liz Davis. He was told she was long gone for the day.

"Can you give me her home phone?" Quist identified himself.

"I'm sorry," the woman on the other end said. "I'm not permitted to give out that number."

"Her home address?"

"I can't give you that either without Miss Davis's permission. She should be here shortly after nine in the morning."

Jerry Collins, the *Journal*'s publisher and editor, didn't answer his home phone, which was listed. Letting time slip by without doing anything was a painful business. At any minute he might get some kind of message, some kind of demand from Lydia's kidnapper that would tie his hands. The longer there was silence from that quarter, the better the possibility that it had no connection with the Bridgetown horrors. Lydia could simply have been grabbed by some mugger on a New York City street, robbed, killed, disposed of. In that case, the killer would never have heard of Quist or anyone on whom he could make a demand. Just another picture in a pattern of terror that stalks the whole world today. Quist kept trying to tell himself that that wasn't it. If Lydia had been taken by the Bridgetown killer, she would be kept alive to force his hand if that became necessary.

He lay, sleepless, on his bed in the suite at Bridgetown House, waiting for Wally, who was still out somewhere electioneering. Then there was sunshine at his window. He had slept. He slipped on a robe and stepped out into the living room. A note was propped up in a conspicuous place on the center table.

"You were asleep when I came in. Didn't want to wake you. Wally."

Quist ordered breakfast from room service and showered, shaved, and dressed for the day. The waiter arrived with the breakfast wagon and Quist sat down to it just as Wally opened the door to his room and looked out, eyes heavy with sleep.

"You saw my note, Julian? It was about four o'clock when I got in and you were really pounding away. I thought I'd let you have it."

"I guess I'm grateful," Quist said.

"Anything about Lydia?"

"No."

Wally chuckled. "Listening to those guys last night, if I believed them I'd think I could be elected president. Any luck with Liz Davis?"

"No. I'm on my way to see her as soon as the business day starts."

Wally's face clouded. "Listening to what Bobby had to say, and you and Dan asking him questions, I have a feeling Martha was involved in something I shouldn't be proud of."

"Don't pass judgment until you have facts," Quist said. "There can be understandable reasons for whatever Martha's lifestyle was. Maybe Liz Davis can help us find out."

At the *Journal* office, a little after nine, Quist was promptly ushered into Liz Davis's office. The lady was at her desk, reading the morning paper. She put it down and pushed her glasses up into her hair.

"I just heard that you were looking for me last night, Julian," she said. "I'm sure you understand why there are instructions here not to give out my number or my address. If that information were available, I'd have half the town yammering at me around the clock. What can I do for you?"

"Tell me what you forgot to tell me yesterday—about your friendship with Martha Best."

Liz Davis's smile was gone. "As the saying goes, what does that have to do with the price of eggs?"

"You talked about her to me as though she were just a news item," Quist said, "not a friend."

"My friendship with Martha had nothing whatever to do with her murder, which is what you and I were talking about."

"Everything about her has something to do with her murder. You were her friend, and you can probably fill in chunks of her life that are missing to Wally, to me, and maybe even to the police."

The lady was silent for a moment, then took a cigarette from a pack on her desk and lit it with a desk lighter. "My friendship with Martha," she said after exhaling a cloud of smoke, "was strictly professional on my side. I got to know her, cultivated that acquaintance, lunched with her a couple of times a week."

"As a reporter and columnist?"

"Yes, although I grew fond of her in the few months our friendship lasted."

"What ended it?"

"Her murder!"

"What value did Martha have to you, professionally?"

"Come on, Julian. Grow up! This town is Manchester Arms, socially, economically, politically. Martha was secretary to the top man. She was an invaluable source of information."

"About social, economic, and political matters?"

"Of course. What else?"

"Scandal? Criminal activities?"

"Oh, come on, Julian. It was no secret that we met for lunch. Quite often Mark Foreman would send a message to me through her—the Argentine ambassador was coming to town to take a tour of the plant and there'd be a big party given for him; Manchester was planning to buy up another Midwestern arms manufacturer; Manchester was looking for a new public relations man. That kind of thing."

The door to the office opened and a young man stepped in. "I'm sorry to crash in, Miss Davis."

"That's all right, Eddie. What is it?"

"A big truck has just arrived in the parking lot," the boy said. "A load of newsprint. Your car is parked in such a way that he can't maneuver into the loading platform. They wondered if you would move it."

Liz Davis reached for her purse and took out her car keys. "Move it for me, will you, Eddie?"

"Sure, Miss Davis. My pleasure."

The boy took the keys and left.

"Where were we, Julian?" Liz asked.

"You were getting tips from Mark Foreman through Martha."

"So, I was grateful for them."

Quist hesitated for a moment. "I don't really know what side of the fence you're on, Liz Davis. But if part of your job is to pay Mark Foreman for tips he sent to you by sending tips of your own, I'm about to provide you with one."

"If that's the way you feel, don't tell me something you don't want passed on." The lady did not sound pleased.

"There was a big blank in Martha's life that Wally couldn't fill, that young people in the city where she grew up couldn't fill. A close woman friend might be able to fill that blank."

"I don't understand. What kind of a blank?"

"Her love life," Quist said.

Liz Davis leaned back in her chair, smiling again. "You think she confided in me?"

"It's just a guess at the moment. I hope you'll tell me. Let me lay it out for you. We have an unusually attractive woman who no longer dates the young men who were longtime friends. She had no public connection with any man that Wally and those friends know about. They thought it might be someone away from Bridgetown, someone she knew before she came back here to work. I think it may have been someone in Manchester Arms who had reasons for keeping it a secret. Martha might have talked to a woman friend, like you, about it."

"Well, she didn't talk to me."

"As a reporter, hasn't it surprised you that no man surfaced at the time of the murder? Didn't it surprise you that no man, who must have known all there was to know about Martha, ever came forward with information?"

Liz Davis hesitated. "Perhaps it did," she said finally. "But no man who loved her would have killed her, moved her body around from place to place."

"She told Wally that she was going to make headlines by blowing Manchester Arms out of the water," Quist said. "If her lover was someone at Manchester Arms, he might have been driven to defend himself and his company."

"I think that's really reaching, Julian," Liz said. "I think—"

She never finished. A violent explosion shook the *Journal* plant. There were sounds of shattering glass, and Quist felt the chair he was in tipping over. There was a clamor of voices from outside the office, and as he scrambled up from the floor Quist saw massive flames shooting up past the windows.

"Let's get out of here!" Liz Davis said.

They went to the office door, and as they opened it, they were met head-on by Jerry Collins, the owner and editor of the paper. Behind him, the office staff was in wild disorder.

"Oh, thank God you're all right, Liz!" Collins said.

"What happened?" Liz asked.

"It was your car," Collins said. "Some kind of a bomb planted in it. I was afraid you were in it!"

"Oh, my God!" Liz said. "Eddie Lukins—"

"What about him?"

"He was moving it for me."

Collins shouted an obscenity, turned, and ran. Liz started to follow him. Quist grabbed her arm and held her. "Don't go down there and expose yourself," he said.

"Why not? Eddie Lukins—"

"Hasn't it percolated?" Quist asked. "That bomb was meant for you, Liz."

PART 3

Chapter One

The parking lot in back of the *Journal* building was a shambles. The car that must have been Liz Davis's was blown to pieces, hot flames shooting skyward. The big tractor trailer truck, loaded with newsprint, was burning fiercely, and a half dozen other cars were involved in lesser fires. Flames crept up one side of the building itself. Sirens shrieked for help.

Half a dozen men stood a little distance from the hot fire that engulfed Liz Davis's car. Obviously there was no way they could help anyone who'd been in the car. Quist watched, shocked by what he saw.

"No chance for the boy," someone said, standing just behind him. Quist turned and saw a white-faced Jerry Collins. "If the bomb was attached to the starter, he never had a chance. He turned the key and—boom!"

"One blessed thing," Quist said. "He never had time to be afraid."

"Nice kid," Collins said. "What we call a 'gofer.' Go for a cup of coffee—go for those papers on my desk. Always happy, smiling."

"It was meant for Liz," Quist said.

"I know. We'll get the son of a bitch who did it if it's the last thing we ever do."

"Why? Why would anyone want to get Liz?" Quist asked.

Collins shrugged. "There are people around who don't like her for something she wrote in her column."

A fire engine plowed into the yard, siren wailing. Collins raced toward the firemen, waving toward the building. It was too late for anything else to matter. Quist turned back into the building. Liz would be wanting to know about the boy. God help him!

Quist, for no sensible reason, found himself unable to accept the possibility that the bombing of Liz Davis's car was not connected to the murders of Sue Wilson and Martha Best. The same kind of psychotic violence made it hard to believe that there were two unrelated terrorists on the loose in Bridgetown.

Liz was standing by the windows of her office, trying to look down at the parking lot through clouds of black smoke. She turned when Quist called out to her, choking from lungs filled with that smoke.

"Eddie?" she managed to ask.

"No chance, I'm afraid," Quist said. "Collins thinks the bomb must have been attached to the starter on your car. If it was, the minute Eddie turned the key—"

"I killed him!" Liz said.

"Don't be absurd," Quist said. "It was his job to run errands. If you had it to do over a hundred times, you'd do it the same way a hundred times. You'd send him down to move your car." Quist waited for her to catch her breath.

"Should we be getting out of here?" she asked.

"Firemen have the building fire under control," Quist said. "I think we should stay put until proper arrangements are made to protect you."

"Protect me?"

"Someone just tried to kill you, Liz. Let's talk about 'why' while we wait."

"But I have no idea!"

"We've both been withholding the truth from each other," Quist said. "You want to keep on that way, it's your choice. I've decided to trust you, so I'll begin by telling you that the story that Lydia—my Lydia Morton—is somewhere in the southwest researching a novel is a fairy story. She's been kidnapped and will be used to stop me in my tracks if I get close to the truth about Martha Best. Once that happens, I won't be able to help you or Wally or anyone else. If you want to take advantage of anything I might be able to do to help, do it now. Once they lower the boom, I'm no use to you or myself."

Liz moved over and sat down behind her desk. She rested her elbows on the flat surface and put her face in her hands.

"Cops will be turning up any minute to find out who had it in for you," Quist said. "Have you decided what you're going to tell them?"

Liz lowered her hands. Her eyes were red and swollen. Smoke or tears? "An innocent boy has to be slaughtered before I can stop dreaming," she said.

"Dreaming?"

She made an extravagant gesture. "The Pulitzer Prize for reporting! I was going to solve the Martha Best murder all by my little self!" Her voice was bitter.

"If you have special information, you'd better give it to the police," Quist said. "Someone knows you're dangerous to them."

"I don't trust the police!" Liz said. "Particularly not Captain Seaton, who's been in charge of the Best case from the start. He could be owned by the killer."

"You want to tell me what you've found?"

Liz brought her fist down on the desk. "I haven't found anything that's solid. It's been a process of elimination."

"Eliminating what?"

She drew a deep breath and settled back in her chair. "I had a reason for thinking the same way you've been thinking—but a better reason than yours," she said. "I had reason to believe that Martha had a lover, someone connected with Manchester Arms. You knew, from Wally, that she was about to expose someone, something connected with Manchester. Because no man has come forward, you begin to ask yourself questions. A girl as attractive as Martha must have had a man. Who was he? Why didn't he come forward after she was killed? Did you never come up with the obvious answer to that?"

"That her man killed her?" Quist asked.

"I had a reason for thinking there was no question about that," Liz said. "The very last time I had lunch with Martha, just a few days before she disappeared in the blizzard, she told me. Not who the man was, but that there was a man, had been a man for the last couple of years. I can hear her words just as clearly as if she were speaking them now. 'Can you imagine what it would be like,' she asked me, 'to be in love with a man for months and months, believe that he was going to break off ties that bound him to someone else, and then discover that he only thought of you as his whore?' I asked her what the ties were that kept her apart from her lover. Was he married? 'Legally, yes,' she told me. 'But I thought he planned to end that.' "

"No name?"

"She just laughed when I asked her. 'But the whole world is going to know when I spread my cards on the table.' "

"Those were the headlines she talked about to Wally?" Quist asked.

"I knew she was badly hurt," Liz said. "I thought her threats were just wild talk. Then came the night of the blizzard, and she disappeared. I thought she'd just run away from her situation. It wasn't until they found her body in the trunk of her car that I knew how far off base I'd been. She'd been silenced, just as you and Wally thought. But the silencer, as far as I was concerned, had to be that man who'd thought of her as his whore, who couldn't risk having her expose him."

"But you never came forward with this."

"They'd had enough time to cover all tracks before they let her be found and we knew she'd been murdered," Liz said. "It seemed certain to me that Martha's man was someone in Manchester Arms. That's where she worked. That's where her life was. If this killer-lover was from Manchester Arms, he'd have an army ready to cover for him. The chief investigators were Bart Havens, head of Manchester's security, and Captain Seaton, who owed his position to Manchester's political pull. I convinced myself that if I started spreading my theory, they'd bury it before I could get it underway. I had to find facts first."

"And you did?"

"No. It's an extraordinary business, Julian. I, in my position as a columnist for the *Journal,* have all kinds of contacts here in Bridgetown. Sure, some of them owe a lot more to Manchester Arms than to me. But somehow one of my sources must have seen or guessed something. A love affair of two years' standing. Where did they meet? Where did they make love, for God's sake? Would you believe that not a single bartender, restaurant owner, gas station attendant would admit ever having seen Martha with any man? No neighbor had heard any gossip about a man coming to her apartment. I couldn't go to Manchester to ask the people who worked there, but they couldn't have spent two years making love at Manchester's plant. I've searched and searched now for six months—for a lead, just for one small whisper! Nothing."

"But you must have come close, or why this?" Quist gestured toward the smoke-clouded window.

"I wish I knew! I wish to God I knew!"

"You want to go over the ground you've covered? Together we might hit on something."

She leaned forward, the corners of her mouth twitching. "I have to tell someone, Julian. If—if I'd gone down to move my own car no one except the killer—and his friends—would know what I've been up to."

"Trust me," Quist said. "I'll help—for as long as I can."

"Of course, the first thing I did was check out the married men in high places at Manchester. Understand, Julian, I didn't think Martha's lover could be some small-time twerp. The cover-up was too elaborate. They kept Martha's body hidden for days while they eliminated any traces there might be. So who was married and in a position of power at Manchester? Mark Foreman, her boss and a known lecher, was the only unmarried man at the top. Seymour Sloan, Jay Thompson, Greg Martin, Ted Devens, Bart Havens—all married. It could be any one of them, I thought. But where was the love affair acted out? Not in Martha's apartment. I had a source there I could trust. No way a lover could have visited there for two years without being seen. A love nest somewhere, out of the country? Martha was seen coming and going from her place at regular times. A cleaning woman who worked for her once a week never saw any traces of a male companion. I drew a blank on where they spent time together."

"Unhappy marriages?" Quist asked.

Liz gave her head a frustrated little shake. "Would you believe bliss everywhere you look? Seymour and Sally Sloan have been married for something like forty years, three grown children, a hat full of grandchildren. Seymour travels quite a lot for Manchester—most of the big boys do. Their business is all over the world. Seymour never goes anywhere without his Sally. It's as if he couldn't get along without Sally to tuck him in at night and wake him up in the morning. They are almost ridiculously inseparable."

"A long-term love affair on the side just not possible?"

"Not thinkable—and I'm talking as a reporter and not a sentimentalist. Seymour Sloan's foot might slip—as any man's or woman's might—but a long love affair on the side? Never."

"How do they differ from the others?"

"Super close," Liz said. "The Thompsons and the Devenses are much the same, if different personalities. Longtime married, children and grandchildren. The Martins and the Havenses are a little different. No children."

"I know a little bit about the Martins," Quist said. "Did a little digging since Greg Martin was going to be running against Wally. Nancy Martin—I met her yesterday at the Women's Rights meeting. She called herself the doorwoman. I understand she is the granddaughter of Herbert Manchester, who founded the arms company."

Liz nodded. "Top of the social ladder, fabulously rich in her own right. Queen bee of Bridgetown society."

"Attractive woman, I thought," Quist said.

"Attractive, generous; sits in, I suspect, on many company decisions. Biggest single stockholder in Manchester Arms."

"And the marriage?"

"Apparently ideal, if you discount the lack of children," Liz said. "They have a big spread just north of town. There are constant parties and charity events. Ask anyone about Greg and Nancy Martin and all you'll hear is applause."

"And the Havenses? Wally and I call him 'that Telly Savalas character.' "

"Different breed of cat," Liz said. "You might say Bart Havens isn't 'one of them.' All the others have grown up in Manchester Arms, their fathers partners of old Herbert Manchester. Havens is a security expert. On one of his trips to the Middle East, Seymour Sloan met Havens, who was working for one of the Arab governments, actually an undercover agent for the British. Manchester Arms was under constant threat of terrorist attack, both abroad and here. Sloan persuaded Havens to take a job with Manchester and come back here to Bridgetown. Apparently he's done a first-class job for Manchester."

"Not at solving Martha's murder," Quist said.

"Nor has anyone else been any good at that—so far," Liz replied.

"His wife?" Quist asked.

"She's an Arab woman," Liz said. "Tanya. I think she is Palestinian. Like most Arab women, she stays strictly in the shadow of her husband. She's rarely seen at any of the social events. But neither is Bart, for that matter. He's a valued employee but not a social friend."

"Tanya Havens wouldn't have stood in the way of a love affair for her husband, just stayed in the shadows?"

"I wrote him off long ago," Liz said, "because Martha talked about him to me. She thought he was 'an arrogant jerk.' I guess, like Mark Foreman, he'd made a pass at her somewhere along the way. She thought it was a sick joke."

"You and Martha were much alike," Quist said. "Attractive, well educated, sophisticated, certainly no trouble attracting men."

"Thank you, sir."

"Which of these men we've been talking about would interest you if he moved your way?"

Liz hesitated. "We've written off Bart Havens. Seymour Sloan is a little too old for my taste. Jay Thompson, just not my type. Ted Devens? I don't think I'd give him a second thought."

"That leaves Greg Martin."

Liz nodded. "You've seen him in action, at the Women's Rights meeting. Nice personality, makes easy contact with groups. He's never given me the eye, but I imagine he'd be equally winning on a one-to-one scale. Understand, I've never given any of these guys a serious thought. But if you asked me to, it would have to be Greg Martin."

"In spite of his glamorous wife?"

"You asked me to choose one of the married men at Manchester. I have had a pass made at me from inside the hallowed halls of Manchester Arms, but he's not married."

"Mark Foreman?"

"I'm not flattered, because any woman who's at all attractive is on his list. Remember what he said about Martha? She said 'No' but not 'Never,' so she must have still been on his list. I said 'Never' the first time around."

"Don't tell me if you don't want to, but who *are* you interested in?" Quist asked.

Liz's face clouded. "An airplane pilot who worked for Manchester," she said. "He died in a crash about two years ago. I haven't gotten over it yet, Julian."

"Sorry. So I think we must stop guessing, lady. Who would want to plant a bomb in your car?"

She shook her head. "It hasn't surfaced yet. Someone crazy I've written something about in the past."

"I still choose to think it's connected to Martha—just as Sue Wilson's death was connected to her. You don't know who Martha's man was. What about Manchester Arms? Have you come up with anything that would damage them if you exposed it?"

"Rumors. Rumors about dealings with countries in the Middle East and Central America that you and I wouldn't think of as friends. But nothing factual, nothing but gossip."

"Still, somebody tried to kill you. How do you propose to protect yourself until we can come up with answers?"

"My God, Julian, I haven't even thought about that. You think—"

"I think they may follow the adage 'If at first you don't succeed, try, try again.' Until you can guess why, you don't know where they'll be coming from. You could leave town, hide out somewhere far away."

Her mouth tightened. "A good journalist doesn't walk out on a story."

Quist hesitated. "You know the Rat Pack kids, Wally's friends? A young man named Bobby Shanks?"

Liz nodded. "Casually. Wally made them famous with his 'Rat Pack Lover' song."

"I could ask them to cover for you. I think they would and not be noticeable. I can stay close only until they use Lydia to stop me."

Liz opened the right-hand drawer of her desk and took out a small-caliber handgun. "I have a license to carry this," she said.

At the same moment, the door to her office opened and Captain Walter Seaton, Bridgetown's homicide specialist, walked in. He glanced at the gun Liz was holding.

"You may need that if you can't give us some kind of a lead, Miss Davis," he said. He turned cold eyes to Quist. "Whenever we have a murder around here lately, you seem to be on deck, Quist."

"I'm not exactly reassured to know that you're in charge of this one," Quist said.

Seaton's smile was more like a grimace. "I understand you were with Miss Davis when the bomb went off. That's a kind of alibi, I suppose. But where were you when the bomb was set in the car? That could have been hours ago."

"Not hours, Captain," Liz said. "I drove that car to work, got here about five minutes after nine. Julian was here with me at about nine-thirty. The bomb went off fifteen minutes later. Whoever planted the bomb did it between five minutes after nine and a quarter to ten."

"Well, at least that's something to go on," Seaton said, scribbling in a pocket notebook.

"Miss Davis is going to need protection until we get a lead to this bomber," Quist said.

"You afraid the Bridgetown police can't protect her?" Seaton asked. "Miss Davis is a pretty popular character around town. People wouldn't be very happy if we let anything happen to her. Now, if you'll take a powder, Quist, I'd like to hear the lady's story."

Liz Davis sat down at her desk and wrote something on a pad of paper. She looked up at Quist when she'd finished writing.

"There's nothing I can tell Captain Seaton that I haven't already told you, Julian." She tore the sheet off the pad and handed it to Quist. "My home address and my unlisted phone. Use either or both if you want to."

Quist took the paper and walked out of the office. He glanced at the paper when he was outside. There was an address and a phone number. There was also a short sentence written below them.

"This man got his job through Manchester's influence."

It was bedlam outside Liz Davis's soundproofed private office. Some of the staff seemed to be involved in a hurried evacuation, emptying the drawers of their desks, removing folders from file cabinets. Others were at phones—reporters, Quist guessed, reporting to their television and radio contacts on the bombing. One or two others stood by the windows, staring down in disbelief at the holocaust in the parking lot.

Out on the street, literally hundreds of people were crowded together, being held at a distance from the *Journal* building by a small army of uniformed police officers. As Quist walked out of the building, people shouted questions at him. "How is it inside?" was the general theme. Then Quist heard his own name being shouted.

"Julian! Julian!"

At the front edge of the held-off crowd was Dan Garvey. Quist walked over to him, and instantly there was no way to hold a private conversation: It seemed that the whole damned city wanted to know what was happening beyond their line of vision.

Garvey took Quist's arm and almost dragged him back through the crowd and finally to something like a clear space.

"Came to find you," Garvey said. "I have news of a sort I wanted to get to you. Whole place seemed to blow up before I could get to you. I understand a kid who was moving a car was killed."

"It was meant for Liz Davis," Quist said. "Lucky for her, horribly bad luck for the kid. If I hadn't been there talking to her, she might have gone to move her car herself."

Garvey steered them into a small lunchroom-type place. The counterman, watching from the front window, didn't even notice them.

They sat down at a corner table, and Garvey reached across and closed his strong fingers on Quist's wrist. "I have some news about Lydia," he said.

Quist was instantly standing.

"Just fasten your seat belt, pal," Garvey said. "It's news, but whether it's good or bad, you'll have to decide for yourself. My friend Sergeant Carter of New York's Missing Persons came up with it."

"Dan, for God's sake, come out with it!"

"Right across from our office in New York," Garvey said, "there is a little store with a newsstand out front. Apparently part of Lydia's routine when she walks to work is to stop at Gardella's for her morning newspaper. Pays for it by the month. Tony Gardella knows her well."

"So?"

"The morning Lydia disappeared, Gardella saw her coming. He was busy with another customer, but he snaked out Lydia's paper for her. When he turned to hand it to her, he saw that she'd stopped down the block to talk to a man. Gardella can describe the guy, all too vaguely, but he says he never saw him before."

"And—?"

"Guy had a car parked at the curb. He went to it, opened the door on the passenger side. Lydia followed him, got into the car. No pressure, no rough stuff. She apparently went quite willingly. Guy walked around the car, got in behind the wheel, and drove off."

"Gardella get the license number?"

"No. Why should he? There didn't appear to be any problem."

"Make of car?"

Garvey shrugged. "Medium-sized sedan, black or dark blue. Gardella thinks it was a two-door job. But understand, Julian, Gardella didn't have any reason to pay special attention. There wasn't any sign of trouble. He just assumed Lydia had met a friend and decided to go somewhere with him—willingly, from all he saw. She'd changed her routine, was all."

"Damn!"

"Sergeant Carter did a very thorough search," Garvey said. "From us he'd learned that she walked to the office from your apartment every day. He checked along the route, doormen at apartment buildings, shopkeepers. He found several who knew Lydia by sight, but none of them could be sure they'd seen her that morning. Maybe, maybe not. But Gardella remembered—some, but not really enough."

"If it was some friend of Lydia's—?"

"She didn't have men friends. Not one who could persuade her to go off for a ride somewhere. Not that day, Julian. You were here in Bridgetown. You might have needed her, although she couldn't have heard about Sue Wilson's murder on her radio. She wouldn't have let herself be out of touch."

"But she went somewhere with someone. Willingly, according to Gardella."

"Suggest anything to you?" Garvey asked, his face grim.

Quist hit the table with the flat of his hand. "It doesn't make any sense."

"If her 'friend' had a message from you?" Garvey asked.

"But I didn't—"

"A con game," Garvey said. "She thought she was being taken to you."

"Taken where?"

"Where else but here in Bridgetown? This guy, whoever he is, has got to be where he's supposed to be."

Guessing, Quist thought. That was all that had been going on in Bridgetown for the last six months, guessing. A guess that Martha Best had had a lover who was high up in Manchester Arms; a guess that that lover was married; a guess that she'd been murdered to stop her from revealing some damaging information about that man or someone else in Manchester Arms. A guess that Sue Wilson had accidentally seen a man she knew in Quist's room at Bridgetown House was another. A guess that Liz Davis was too close to something she didn't realize was dangerous was another. Now there was a guess that Lydia had been brought here to Bridgetown to be used to stop Quist and Garvey if they got anywhere near a damaging fact. Guesses, guesses, guesses!

"We're here to handle Wally Best's political campaign," Garvey said. "As long as that's all we do, Lydia may be safe. If they think we're moving any other way . . ." He let it rest there.

Quist stood up again. "I'm pulling out of this," he said. "The only thing in the world that matters a damn to me, Dan, is Lydia. If pulling out will set her free, then I'm gone. We're gone!"

Garvey didn't move. "Can this bastard risk setting her free then, or ever? She knows who the man was who picked her up in New York with some kind of a con story. She knows who her jailer is now, feeding her, keeping the door locked on her."

Quist's voice wasn't steady. "Then why is he keeping her alive?"

"Hearing from her, live on the phone, would stop you in your tracks," Garvey said. "Start moving toward him and he'll use that final weapon. But that doesn't mean he'll let her go after that."

"You're saying—?"

"That Lydia's chances aren't too good whatever you do, Julian. I'm sorry to say it, but that's the way it looks to me. Back off, and they won't need to keep Lydia alive to use as a weapon anymore. Stay put, promote Wally Best's campaign, which is what you came here for, and they may keep her alive—just in case. She's not dangerous to them, Julian, until she can talk to someone outside their world. She could be useful in case you get accidentally lucky."

"So how do we get 'accidentally lucky'?"

"There's a starting point that occurs to me," Garvey said. "Lydia was last seen alive Wednesday morning, just before nine o'clock, by Tony Gardella, the newspaper guy. Whoever conned Lydia was there, of course, with his car. So he couldn't have been here. So who wasn't here who should have been?"

"So we start asking people where they were at nine o'clock on Wednesday morning and they know we're not promoting Wally Best's campaign," Quist said.

"Not you, not me," Garvey said. "Maybe Bobby Shanks and his Rat Pack friends. Your Liz Davis may have people who'd nose around for her. We have to think that Davis is on our side after what's just happened. There's one other possibility. Persuade this Gardella guy to come up here. Let him hang around Manchester Arms watching the comings and goings. Maybe he'd recognize the guy he saw drive Lydia off in his car. That would be better than sitting around waiting for them to pass a death sentence on Lydia."

Quist sat down again, took a deep breath, and let it out slowly. "Thanks for being you, Dan," he said.

Chapter Two

It was not an easy matter that morning to distract a Bridgetown resident's attention from what had happened at the *Journal.* Eddie Lukins, the boy killed in the explosion, was the son of Tom Lukins, who ran a machine shop on River Street. Long ago, Tom's father had operated a blacksmith shop on that site.

The Lukinses were a part of Bridgetown's history. A few old-timers would offer genuine sympathy to Tom and Amanda Lukins over the tragic death of their young son, but the majority of Bridgetowners were excited about who the intended victim had been. Everyone who read the *Bridgetown Journal* turned to Liz Davis's "Up and Around" column after only the briefest glance at the headlines. Headlines weren't often very important in the *Journal*, but tomorrow's would be; a bomb set in Liz Davis's car, intended to kill her!

Liz Davis had been referred to by her boss, Jerry Collins, as "Bridgetown's conscience." This sophisticated, often witty reporter was a repository for dozens of secrets about Bridgetown's inner life. She wasn't a gossip, so she didn't report what "might be," but she certainly knew things that a great many people hoped would never appear in print. Someone must have felt threatened, but who, and why? Could she be telling the police now whom she suspected? Would tomorrow's paper rip the cover off some hidden Bridgetown scandal?

Quist thought he knew what was under that cover. Liz Davis had been flirting with the truth about Martha Best, who Martha's lover and murderer might be, who had killed Sue Wilson at Bridgetown House. If she didn't tell Captain Seaton now whom she suspected, how long would she be safe? If she did tell him, how long would she be safe? If Seaton was a pawn in Manchester Arms' scheme of things, as she'd suggested in her note to Quist, she was under the gun, as was Lydia! Violence was bubbling in a cauldron of hate somewhere close by.

Garvey had taken off to get in touch with his friend Sergeant Carter in New York, with the hope that Tony Gardella, the man who'd seen Lydia drive off with a stranger, could be persuaded to come to Bridgetown to try to identify that man. Money was no object, if that was needed, to persuade Gardella to cooperate. Quist was to look for Bobby Shanks with the chance that the Rat Pack boys might come up with who had been absent from Bridgetown the morning that Lydia had disappeared, someone connected with Manchester Arms. With smoke still pouring out of the parking lot behind the *Journal* building, the best chance of finding anyone was right here on the spot. Shanks and his friends, along with dozens of others, were probably circulating here, waiting for some kind of solid information about the bombing and murder. Finding one special person in this crowd of excited onlookers was a needle-in-a-haystack puzzle. Quist was hampered by the fact that he'd been seen coming out of the building after the bomb had exploded, and a hundred people had had a hundred questions for him. He couldn't move two feet without being stopped by someone.

He felt a strong hand close on his arm from behind, heard his name spoken in an authoritative voice. He turned and found himself facing Mark Foreman, the president of Manchester Arms.

"Can we get out of this crazy house and go somewhere to talk?" Foreman asked.

"This is surely not the time to discuss a political campaign," Quist said.

"Who the hell wants to talk about a political campaign?" Foreman asked. "My car's just a half a block away. Will you come?"

Foreman, his dark face a grim thundercloud, didn't wait for an answer. He moved through the crowd, growling an occasional order to "Make way." His face was probably as familiar in Bridgetown as George Washington's. He was "The Man," and even if people resented being told what to do, they did what they were told.

Quist followed Foreman. The key man at Manchester Arms could be invaluable, could have the answers Quist badly wanted. Whether he would provide those answers was another matter. At least he was the one who wanted to talk, which tilted things a little bit Quist's way.

Foreman's Mercedes was parked on a side street. A boy was sitting on the curb beside it. He stood up as Foreman approached.

"Any problems, Joey?" Foreman asked.

"No, sir."

"Thanks for keeping an eye on her for me." Foreman handed the boy a bill. Quist couldn't see what the denomination of the bill was. Foreman gestured to the passenger side, and Quist got in. Foreman got behind the wheel and started the car's motor.

"Friend of mine has a cottage a few blocks away," he said. "Nice garden where we can sit and talk."

"About what?" Quist asked.

Foreman's mouth twisted in a bitter smile. "I'm the man who's supposed to know everything that's going on in my world," he said, "from whether my yard man's dog has worms to what the mayor had for breakfast. Head up a multinational corporation and you can't have any secrets kept from you."

"Am I supposed to have secrets I'm keeping from you?"

"Maybe," Foreman said. "More likely we can help each other come up with answers neither of us has at the moment."

"Answers to what?"

"Murder!" Foreman said. "Three of them, unsolved, are cluttering up my world. Two more could be waiting just around the corner."

"Two more?"

"The Lukins boy was an accident. That bomb this morning was meant for Liz Davis. Someone will probably try again. Then there's your Miss Morton."

Quist felt his heart slam against his ribs. "You know about her?" he asked, his voice suddenly unsteady.

"Old friend of mine, Sergeant Jake Carter of Manhattan's Missing Persons Bureau," Foreman said. "He's found a half dozen people for me over the years. He called to ask me for help in finding your lady. You've suddenly moved into my world, Quist. Whatever you may say, I know you're in Bridgetown to try to track down Martha Best's killer. I know this campaign of Wally's is just a front. Then Sue Wilson is murdered in your hotel room. You were with Liz Davis when someone tried to get her. Your lady has been kidnapped to be used as a weapon against you. It's time you and I joined forces, Quist, if we don't want more murders on our hands, and old ones unsolved."

The car turned off the main street and onto a country road. At the end of it was a small white cottage with a pretty little garden to one side of it, looking down over the silver strip that was the Hudson River, far below. Foreman got out of the car, but Quist didn't move. He felt frozen there. Was this man on the level, or was he about to be warned what would happen to Lydia if he didn't obey orders?

"Every minute we waste may be fatal to someone," Foreman said as he opened the door on the passenger side.

Quist moved realizing that all of the bones in his body were stiff. Terrible fear for Lydia made it difficult for him to breathe. Foreman led the way down to a couple of white iron garden chairs placed in the shade of a handsome old maple tree.

"My friend's away," Foreman said. "We won't be interrupted here. You don't trust me, do you?"

"If you know as much as you say you do, then you know that I can't trust anyone," Quist said.

"From what you know it must be obvious to you that I can't trust anyone either," Foreman said. "You're my best hope."

"You want to start with what you know?" Quist asked. "Like who was Martha Best's lover?"

Foreman's mouth thinned into a straight, hard line. "If I knew that, Sue Wilson and the Lukins boy would be alive, and Liz Davis and Miss Morton would be safe."

"Martha worked for you for what, about four years? She had no boyfriend that anyone admits knowing about. One has to believe that she was having an affair with someone who had to keep it secret. A married man? You know whether your yard man's dog has worms and what the mayor had for breakfast, but you don't know who Martha was in bed with, though I was told she worked with you every day of your life except Sundays?"

"A weakness, based on a weakness," Foreman said.

"Would you like to explain that?"

"I'm not married," Foreman said. "Divorced a long time ago. I head a big company with a lot of social life going on that is part of the business. I—I have an appetite for women. I don't want commitments or permanence. It doesn't matter to me if the lady is attractive, whether she's married or single. In my world most of them turn out to be married. What goes on between me and a lady is nobody's business but ours. Nothing could persuade me to kiss and tell. I don't expect other people to tell me about their lives. It's their private life. If they're in my company, as long as they do their job for me, what they do in private, in bed, they're entitled to keep to themselves. It's what I want for me. I give it to them."

"But you can't stop wondering or guessing, can you?" Quist asked.

"I suppose not, but I don't dig," Foreman said. "You're talking about Martha. Yes, I was curious about her. She was an attractive, sexy lady. I told you the first time we met that I'd made a pass at her. She said no, obviously involved with someone else."

"But not 'Never,' you told me."

"It may have been her way of flirting, suggesting that sometime later she might respond differently. But she never did."

"And as time went on, you never had a clue who the man was she was saying 'Yes' to?"

Foreman shrugged. "I tell you, I wanted to be private. I respect other people's desire for privacy."

Quist changed direction. "Martha, according to all reports, was a top-drawer secretary."

"The best."

"Would it surprise you to hear that she told Wally, just a couple of weeks before she was murdered, that she was about to reveal secrets that could be damaging to Manchester Arms?"

"Manchester Arms, or someone working for Manchester Arms?" Foreman asked.

"I'm quoting what Wally says his sister told him," Quist said. "I didn't hear it myself."

Foreman reached into his pocket and took out a leather cigar case. He took a long, thin cigar from it and lit it. "You want to take a minute to imagine what it's like to be selling weapons of war, weapons that can be used in a campaign of terror, on the open market? No matter who you sell to, there are people who will think it's a criminal act, in a moral sense. Manchester Arms doesn't sell who it's illegal to sell to. We don't sell to street-corner gangsters. But let us say we sell to Israel. Right away the whole Arab world and a few hundred thousand anti-Semites around the globe start yelling 'Foul!' We sell arms to Israel, and the next day we sell arms to Syria. It's legal. They buy in the open market. But now the Syrians are yelling 'Foul!' and the Israelis are yelling 'Foul!' Then there are millions of moralists who say we should not be selling arms to anyone. You know who our best customer is? Uncle Sam! But those moralists will tell you we shouldn't be selling arms to the United States. So the Russians can run over us and enslave us? In my business, Quist, there's always someone who thinks we're committing a crime."

"But Martha Best, who worked for you, knew all that," Quist said. "What could she have been talking about?"

Foreman's strong white teeth bit down on his cigar. "That's what I need to find out, Quist, and in a hurry. It could save Liz Davis, and Miss Morton, and God knows who else who might know what Martha meant."

"You'd protect your key people?" Quist asked.

"From a mistake, yes. From deliberate treachery to my company, never. Like what I do or not, Quist, you'll find out—if you can't accept my word for it—that I don't break the law, nor do I allow the people who work for me to break the law."

"What else could you say?"

Impatience crept into Foreman's manner. "Yesterday at that women's meeting I offered Wally Best and his people, including you, access to our books, files, records. That offer still stands."

"You could have disposed of anything that would be damaging to you long before you made that offer," Quist said.

"Yes, we could have, but we didn't." Foreman bit down hard on his cigar again. "Those files and records are open to any of my key people."

"And those key people are—?"

"Seymour Sloan, Greg Martin, Jay Thompson, Ted Devens," Foreman said.

"Your Telly Savalas security chief?"

"Bart Havens? He does look like Telly, doesn't he? Yes, he had access."

"Martha Best, while she was working for you?"

"All she had to do was pull open a file drawer and look," Foreman said. "Nothing is kept under lock and key. The only people who wouldn't have access are the press and our competitors in the arms field."

"But Martha had something that would be damaging, she told Wally."

Foreman's smile was mirthless. "If she had something, she found it out in bed," he said. He moved restlessly in his chair. "I'd hoped we might be able to join forces, Quist. If you're not willing, forget it and let's stop wasting time."

Quist sat silent for a moment. Logic told him not to trust this man, but he had a gut feeling that he should play along. Until Lydia was directly threatened, he couldn't miss the chance to be on the inside for a while.

"I'll go with you," he said.

"No secrets from each other?" Foreman said.

"I wish I had a secret to keep from anyone," Quist said.

Foreman glanced at his wrist watch. "I have a regular morning meeting of the top brass in my office in about twenty minutes," he said. "Let's get moving."

When Quist and Foreman arrived at the office of the president of Manchester Arms, the others were all there, waiting: Sloan, Martin, Thompson, Devens, the shaven-headed Bart Havens, and Betsy Holden, Foreman's secretary, who'd had such good things to say about Martha Best, her predecessor. All of them were mainly concerned about the bombing at the *Jour-*

nal. They seemed to assume that Foreman had brought Quist with him because he'd been with Liz Davis when the bomb went off and might know something that wasn't yet general knowledge.

"Liz give you any hint as to why?" Seymour Sloan asked.

"It was so sudden she didn't have time to gather her wits," Quist said. "She was in shock over having sent the Lukins boy down to move her car and cost him his life. Then Captain Seaton was there and I was given the gate."

"Let's put the cards on the table, gentlemen," Foreman said. "We've got to face the fact that what's going on in this town is not a series of coincidences. It starts with Martha's murder. I don't imagine any of us has been gullible enough to believe that Wally Best really wants to be mayor of Bridgetown. He came here with Quist to find his sister's killer. That's why his room and Quist's were searched. They might have had something that would be dangerous to that killer. Sue Wilson caught him red-handed, and he killed her. Liz Davis, a first-rate reporter, must also have been trying to find answers that the rest of us have missed. She was meant to be next—and may still be next if she doesn't tell Captain Seaton what she has."

And she wouldn't tell Seaton, Quist knew. Her note to him indicated that she didn't trust Seaton, wouldn't tell him anything—if there were something.

"I brought Quist here with me," Foreman said, "because he needs each of you to answer a question."

"What kind of a question?" Greg Martin asked.

"Where were each of you at a few minutes before nine o'clock last Wednesday morning?"

So he was going to spill it, Quist thought. If one of the people in this room was responsible for what had happened to Lydia, he was about to be warned. The threat to Lydia could be just around the corner.

They all acted puzzled.

"We were all here for this regular meeting at ten o'clock," Seymour Sloan said. "Before that, a regular morning for me. Breakfast with my wife, papers on the Saudi Arabian deal I needed to refresh myself on before the meeting. I stopped for gas and an oil check at Fuller's gas station on the way in. What's supposed to have happened at nine o'clock?"

Foreman ignored the question. "You, Greg?"

"I was here at a little after nine," Greg Martin said. "I'd set up a meeting with Perry Lewis to discuss my campaign strategy." He glanced at Quist. "Lewis is my campaign manager. I was here till the ten o'clock meeting started. What is this, Mark? What has nine o'clock Wednesday morning got to do with anything?"

Foreman glanced at Quist. "Want to tell them?"

One of them knew, Quist thought. The others might just turn out to be helpful. It was too late to stall the one who knew.

"My partner, and, it is no secret, the lady in my life, was kidnapped in New York a few minutes before nine on Wednesday," Quist said. "We're assuming that she will be used to stop me if I get somewhere near the truth about Martha Best's murder, and Sue Wilson's, and Eddie Lukins's."

Jay Thompson shook his head as if he couldn't believe what he'd heard. "You think one of us is a murderer, Quist? Let me point out one thing to you. There's no way in the world someone could have been committing a crime at nine o'clock in New York and been back here for a ten o'clock meeting. It's a two-hour drive, an hour-and-a-half if you exceed the speed limit."

There was a chorus of agreement.

"A plane or helicopter?" Quist suggested.

"With your lady as a prisoner?" Martin asked. "None of us fly privately. A trip with an unwilling prisoner would be just about impossible. There'd be a pilot, people at airports on both ends. That's just not sensible, Quist."

"Let's clear it up," Foreman said.

Thompson always started late for the office on Wednesdays. The morning in question he'd driven his wife to the hairdresser. Ted Devens had stopped at the barber's on his way to work. There'd be witnesses to that.

"And you, Bart?" Foreman asked.

The security man rubbed his shaven head and gave them a broad grin. "I'm 'It', I guess," he said. "Sue Wilson's murder wasn't Manchester Arms' business, but since it involved Wally Best and Quist here, I had a feeling we needed to know more about it. I didn't come directly in. I was hanging around the hotel, talking to some street people who are contacts."

"You didn't come to that meeting, did you, Bart, that Wednesday?" Foreman asked.

"No, I didn't," Havens said. "But I'm not required to be here, boss, unless you have something special to pass on to me. I suppose I can dig up enough witnesses to satisfy Quist."

"You do that," Foreman said.

"One thing's certain, though," Havens said. "If this kidnapper is the guy who killed Martha Best, I'm *not* 'It'! I was out of the country the night of the blizzard. Remember, Mr. Foreman? You sent me down to Venezuela to talk to the *contras* down there about a sale of rifles. You sent me because I knew one of the revolution leaders personally—a one-time cop on the police force here."

"I remember," Foreman said. "I guess that's it, Quist."

Quist felt his body begin to tremble. "I just want to say," he said, "that if Lydia Morton is harmed or killed, somebody is going to die for it at my hands!"

There was a murmur of voices that sounded almost sympathetic. Looking around at the men, Quist found himself assailed by doubts. Had one of these men been Martha Best's lover? Sloan, Thompson, and Devens, old enough to be her father. Martin at least ten years older and married to a glamorous lady who was a big stockholder in Manchester Arms. Havens just not believable. Could he be way down the wrong street? Sloan, Martin, Thompson, and Devens could not have been in New York on Wednesday morning. Havens could probably prove he hadn't been. Of course, these were all men who could have hired someone outside their own world who could have abducted Lydia. They had the money, probably the contacts. Where, in God's name, to start if that were the case?

"I think we're entitled to know why Mr. Quist thinks we in this room can be involved in murder and the abduction of Miss Morton," Seymour Sloan said. Iron-gray hair, heavy black eyebrows, and pale blue eyes made him a formidable-looking figure. He could be called handsome, but Martha's lover? Unless there was something very special below the surface—

"There's no reason to be secret about it," Foreman said. "If I were in his shoes, I'd be thinking the way he's thinking. It just happens I know you people a hell of a lot better than he does."

"So why does he suspect us of something?" Ted Devens asked. His faded brown hair was carefully brushed over a bald spot, Quist saw. He might be a genius at automatic weapons, but the lover of a beautiful young woman? Not likely.

"Martha Best had a kind of mystery in her life, at least as far as I was concerned," Foreman said.

"I know," Jay Thompson said. "No guy! I was curious, but after she'd been here a couple of years I explained it to myself."

"Oh?" Foreman said.

Thompson nodded. "Queer. Lesbian. Only explanation for a doll like Martha to be running around without a man."

"Unless the man had to keep it a secret from a jealous wife," Foreman said.

"Mr. Thompson's guess that Martha was queer is way off target," Quist said. "I knew her quite well when we were first promoting Wally. Young men swarmed around her like flies."

"Older men would probably sense it sooner," Thompson said. "Not waste their time dreaming about her."

"I can throw a little confusion into that argument, Jay," Bart Havens said. The security man gave his professional grin. "Early stages after Martha was killed, I was doing everything I could to get my hooks into something. Who were her friends, in and out of the office? Everyone liked her, but no one was close. No one came up easily with some guy's name. You'd expect that, you know? But she didn't seem to have any close girlfriend, not here in the office, at any rate."

"So she was just nonsexual," Thompson suggested.

"I found out from the local drugstore that she was on the pill," Havens said. "If she wasn't having sex with a man, why would she be concerned about birth control?"

"The music goes round and round," Greg Martin said. "A mysterious lover somewhere."

"Right here in this room?" Foreman asked.

Jay Thompson laughed. "We haven't had any romances in this office since Greg and Nancy lit up the town a few years back."

"One of the things that sometimes make it dull around here," Seymour Sloan said. "No gossip."

They were brushing it off, Quist thought.

"Sooner or later you may all have to check out your alibis for Wednesday morning," Foreman said. "Quist can't stay away from the police too long." He turned directly to Quist. "I think you're looking in the wrong place for your Miss Morton. We'll do what we can to prove it to you."

"There are a couple of dozen young men in this office who could have been interested in Martha Best," Greg Martin said.

"And hide it?" Foreman asked. "I know I wouldn't have if I'd been that lucky. Guys wear a girl like Martha like a medal."

"But whoever he was, he didn't," Quist said.

It was like an acute chronic pain that wouldn't go away. Lydia's chances were growing slimmer by the minute, Quist told himself. If the man responsible for her disappearance had been in Foreman's office just now, he was warned; he could be fully prepared. He'd know every step that was being taken to find Lydia, and he'd know just how long it would be safe to keep her alive. There would be a phone call, the sound of her voice warning him off, and then silence forever. How to counterattack before it was too late?

The confusion outside the *Journal* building hadn't subsided when Quist returned there. He had to believe that Liz wouldn't have left her office. This was too big a news story for her to pass up, even though it involved a life—the threat to hers.

Cops were guarding all the entrances, and no one was to be admitted without special authorization from Captain Seaton or Jerry Collins, the publisher and editor. Quist had to stand in line to get to one of the phone booths outside the building. When it was finally his turn, he called Liz's office, got a strange woman's voice, identified himself, and was finally connected with Liz.

"Are you all right?"

Her laugh was thin. "Do you mean have I stopped shaking? Yes, I'm all right—after a fashion."

"Can you spare me a little time?" Quist asked. "I've just come from Foreman's office, where all the top brass at Manchester Arms were gathered."

"This thing is cooking like an egg on a hot stove," Liz said. "I can't leave it for long. But come to the side entrance. I'll send someone down to get you in."

"Captain Seaton still with you?"

"The captain didn't find me too useful," Liz said.

At the side entrance a uniformed cop was ready for Quist and let him in. Inside the building, the confusion was almost as great as it was out on the street. Elevators were crowded, and Quist finally walked up the three flights of stairs to Liz's office. A cop blocked his way until he could prove who he was. Inside, Liz was at her desk, bed-sheet white but apparently functioning. She gestured him to a chair while she completed a phone call.

"If you've ever been shot at," she said, as she put down the receiver, "you'll know how I'm feeling. I've been trying to find out what I can do for Eddie Lukins's family, God help them. For them it's as if he'd been killed by a hit-and-run driver."

"I need to catch you up," Quist said.

He told her the whole story of his encounter with Foreman, the truth about Lydia, and the conference with the big shots. Liz listened, leaning back in her chair, hands locked in front of her, knuckles showing white.

"So you blew it all to them," she said.

"It may sound crazy to you," Quist said, "but I had a gut feeling about Foreman. If anyone on the inside could be helpful, it might be him. After all, he came to me; I didn't go to him."

"He's not likely to have been Martha's lover," Liz said. "He'd have had no reason to hide it."

"But everyone knows why I'm really in Bridgetown, and the man who has Lydia has been alerted."

"You still think you've just been face to face with the killer?"

"I have no other place to go," Quist said, "unless you have an explanation for the bomb that will head me in another direction. And I have no time left, Liz, if Lydia is to have any chance at all."

Liz sat very still, her hands still locked in front of her. "In a madhouse like this," she said finally, "you'd hardly dare talk to your own mother. But you're the one person I know, Julian, along with Wally and your partner, Dan Garvey, who has anything more than a straightforward axe to grind. None of you were involved when all this started. You have no reason to be interested in anything but the truth."

"Are you trying to sell yourself on that?" Quist asked.

"I suppose. In any event, I'm going to tell you what's on my mind."

"Please—if it will move us in the right direction."

Liz unlocked her hands and rubbed them together to get the circulation going. "The day Martha Best was reported missing, and certainly the day her body was found in the trunk of her car, she became the main news story in Bridgetown."

"Naturally."

"A murderer knows the cops are searching for him," Liz said. "He also knows that every competent reporter in town is looking for him, too. If he has his ear to the keyhole, he knows who asks what questions. He knows, in short, whether the trail is staying cold or whether it's heating up."

"In short, someone thought you were getting awfully damn close," Quist said.

Liz nodded. "But, unfortunately, that's not true. I have some theories but no facts to support them."

"But after the bomb, you have to know you are getting close."

Liz leaned forward. "What would you do, in my position as a local resident and a reporter for the local paper, if you thought you had a lead to a killer?"

"Go to the police with it, I suppose."

"I haven't done that. Can you guess why?"

"Cynically—because you want to scoop the area press, and the national television and radio networks. Wally Best's involvement makes it a big story."

"Guess again," Liz said.

"You don't have enough yet."

Liz nodded. "I don't suppose you can walk into a town like this, a stranger, and even guess at all the complexities of its life pattern. Who has what job? How did he get it? Who are his friends? How does he relate to the power structure? You'd have to learn who's who before you'd be able to guess at what's what."

"So tell me, what's what?" Quist said.

Liz nodded again. "There are some interesting things about the Martha Best case. First of all, she's missing after a blizzard. So are other people. Nobody worries about it until the night of the next day when Mark Foreman starts asking about her. A couple of days pass. The police search her apartment, search her car where it has been impounded. Nothing. Then a private eye who Wally hired starts over again and finds the body in the car."

"Ancient history," Quist said.

"Captain Seaton searched the apartment and the car first. If there was any evidence in the apartment, he must have found it. He says there was nothing. No fingerprints on the car, no body. But the car is parked in a police lot. Somebody takes the body there and puts it in Martha's car. Who could go into that lot without attracting attention? Who could have access to the car keys that would unlock its trunk?"

Quist sat very still. "Are you suggesting—?"

"A cop!" Liz said. "Who doesn't have to have an alibi for any time or any place? A cop! Who could walk into the parking lot after I'd gone to work this morning and look like a part of the scenery? A cop! But before this morning, I'd started to walk down that path. Captain Seaton got to the top of the heap in the Bridgetown police department by doing favors for the big shots in Manchester Arms. That's no secret. It occurred to me, before this morning, that Seaton could be persuaded—or bought—to cover for someone in Manchester Arms. I ask a few questions about times and places and I'm ticketed for assassination!"

"You think—?"

"I think there's money enough to tempt a man like Seaton to cover up a crime for a powerful friend. I think I've gotten too inquisitive for him."

"Seaton could have had all the time he needed to cover all traces."

"A cop is invisible—in a way," Liz said. "He's entitled to be anywhere, so no one pays any particular attention when he turns up somewhere. He could have been down here in the parking lot, planting that bomb in my car, and no one would have interfered. They might wonder what he was doing there, but they wouldn't question his right to be there."

"Sue Wilson must have questioned his right to be searching my room at Bridgetown House," Quist said.

"True—and I wonder why, if Seaton is our man."

"How could he have guessed that you had begun to suspect him?" Quist asked.

"Because I'm a damned fool with a big mouth," Liz said, sounding angry. "Would you believe—I was a guest speaker at one of Maggie Nolan's women's groups a few days ago. My talk was about what makes a good reporter. In a question period after my speech, everyone was interested in the Martha Best case. Wally and you had come to town to launch his campaign for mayor. I don't remember how it came up, but I found myself going into my theory about the 'invisible villain,' someone who had a right to be somewhere and wouldn't be questioned about it. The janitor of a building wouldn't have to explain why he was in his building at any unusual time; a trackwalker could be anywhere along a railroad line and no one would question his right. Someone suggested that a cop could be anywhere at all, and no one would question his right to be there. 'Perfect job for a crook,' I remember saying. It started me thinking. If the killer was someone in Manchester Arms, Walter Seaton was someone who might help him stay undercover. I asked a few questions here and there—and I just missed being blown to pieces this morning."

"But you don't have any solid evidence?"

"Not yet," Liz said. "And if I keep looking for something solid, I'm likely to get it from some other direction."

"And you can't go to Seaton with all this because he may be the man."

"Right. And one more thing, Julian. How to find out where Seaton was at nine o'clock on Wednesday morning. Maybe someone can alibi him, but he could have been in New York, waiting outside your office for Lydia Morton to come to work. He could easily have persuaded her to get into his car and head back up here with him. He'd have his police badge, other credentials. He tells Lydia you need her here, so she gets into his car with him. There are hundreds of places here where he could hide her."

"If he means to keep her alive," Quist said.

"Why else would he take her unless he could use her to stop you at some point?"

"Dan Garvey is trying to get a newsstand man who saw Lydia drive away with a stranger to come up here and look for that stranger."

"If he comes, have him get a look at Captain Seaton. But if Seaton's the man, have them play it very cool. Seaton could still lead you to where he's hiding Lydia if he doesn't guess you've identified him."

Chapter Three

The impulse to go to Seaton and wring the truth out of him was almost irresistible. But Seaton, if he were the man, would almost certainly never talk. One of them would wind up dead, and Liz Davis might not live long enough to report her suspicions. A dead Seaton couldn't tell them where Lydia was being held. There was someone at Manchester Arms who was Seaton's man who must know where Lydia was and who'd be ready to deal with her if something happened to Seaton.

From a phone booth, Quist called his office in New York and got his secretary, Connie Parmalee, on the line. Dan Garvey, he was told, had phoned the office but hadn't arrived yet. Bobby Hilliard, his young partner, had been sent to contact Tony Gardella, the newsstand man, with instructions to tell Gardella he could name his own price for coming up to Bridgetown with Garvey.

"But Dan won't make it here for another hour—very little less," Connie said. "Discussion with Gardella, another couple of hours to get back to Bridgetown if Gardella is persuaded. Anything up there, Julian?"

"We've got someone for Gardella to look at," Quist said.

"Good luck. If there's anything at all we can do here—"

"I know. If there is I'll be in touch."

"The Davis woman is okay?"

"So far," Quist said. "A boy is dead, however. And Lydia—"

"If you haven't heard from her, she has to be alive, Julian. That's why she was taken—to be used against you."

"I pray while I wait," Quist said.

Was this something he dared share with Bobby Shanks, Wally's Rat Pack friend? It was too risky to trust just anyone. A slip of the tongue, an overt action of some kind, and the curtain would lower on Lydia before Gardella had a chance to say yes or no about Captain Seaton. Wally was the one person still in

Bridgetown whom he could trust. He shouldn't be too hard to find. Thousands of people knew him by sight. Quist didn't want to risk leaving a message at Bridgetown House—or should he? Too many people there were under too many dangerous thumbs.

Questions in the street. "Have you seen Wally Best?" "He was just over there—just over there." Wally had been seen everywhere and was momentarily nowhere.

Standing in the phone booth, Quist noticed the local telephone directory. Walter Seaton was listed, not as a policeman, just as "Seaton, Walter." Quist scribbled down the address and went out to find the place where Seaton lived. He hoped for an isolated cottage, shared by no one, where Lydia could be held in secret. It turned out to be in the dead center of town, a red brick apartment building where, according to the bell panel in the foyer, at least six families lived. No place to hold a prisoner who wasn't bound, gagged, and tied down!

An elderly woman mopping down the front hall answered Quist's questions without any embarrassment. Yes, Captain Seaton of the local police lived here—Apartment Three A. No, he wasn't in.

"I just finished cleaning his apartment," the woman said.

"No one up there?"

"No. He goes to work before I turn up in the morning, and I'm long gone before he gets home in the afternoon. I see him on Sundays when he pays me for the week."

"But you clean his apartment every weekday?"

"Yes, sir—if it's any of your business."

Loyalty at best—or worst, Quist thought. There was no excuse he could offer for asking for a look at Seaton's apartment.

Time moved with a painful slowness. It would be late afternoon before Dan could get back with Gardella—if Gardella would come. Wally seemed to have disappeared in a puff of smoke. Somewhere Lydia was waiting for what she must know was the end of the line. That couldn't happen to someone in the real world! Maybe in a novel or a movie plot, but not in the real world—but it was happening.

Looking around, Quist realized he'd wandered back close to the Manchester Arms plant. The man who had murdered Martha Best was inside those walls, he thought to himself, the man who may have enlisted the help of Captain Seaton, the man who was playing games with the life of the most precious person in the world, Lydia.

A terrible anger was eating at Quist. He should go in there, tear them all apart, one by one, until one of them screamed for mercy and told him where Lydia was. What was the use of waiting for Gardella to finger Captain Seaton? When that was done, if it was done, what was the next move? Could you go to the local police, where Seaton rated near the top? They would be laughing at him while Seaton took off to make sure Lydia was never found.

He turned toward the plant and found himself face to face with Betsy Holden, Mark Foreman's secretary.

"Mr. Quist! Can I do anything for you?"

Quist drew a deep breath. "I wish you could. I wish I knew what to ask for."

"This is a town of tragedies. It must be an ugly place for you," the girl said. "Mr. Foreman told me about your missing lady. No news of her?"

"Nothing, and no lead to anything," Quist said. And then it suddenly occurred to him that there might be a way this girl could help—if she weren't a party to the whole conspiracy, too. "One of my problems is that I got off on the wrong foot with Captain Seaton, who's in charge of the case. I let him know I thought he'd blundered in Martha Best's murder, and now I can't go to him for help."

"Seaton isn't the easiest man in the world for anyone to get along with," Betsy Holden said. "He's a kind of a chippy fellow."

"Chippy?"

"Chip on his shoulder," Betsy said.

"I understand he's very well thought of by your people."

"In a way, I suppose he owes his job to us."

"How's that?"

"Strange thing," Betsy said. "Manchester needs a very special kind of man to handle security. People who are dangerous to us come from all parts of a sick world that is dominated by terrorists these days. We need a man who can deal with that kind of violent situation without hesitating. The best choices would come from people who've had experience in the Middle East, or Central America, or Cuba—or what-have-you. Our directors, who travel overseas to visit with our customers in those places, often come up with the kind of man we need. A couple of years back—before my time—our head man died in what may or may not have been an accident. His house burned to the ground, and he never got out. Mr. Sloan, I'm told, came back from abroad with Bart Havens. At the same time, Mr. Thompson produced Walter Seaton, whom he'd found in Spain, I believe, where he was working in the American embassy. Mr. Foreman had to make a choice between Havens and Seaton. He chose Havens. Mr. Thompson felt he owed Seaton something and used his influence to get him a job on the local police force. I guess he was good at it, because he was very quickly in charge of Homicide. He's always been ready to do anything Manchester wanted from him, particularly Mr. Thompson."

Jay Thompson, in his early sixties, once-dark hair almost white, arthritic fingers that he was constantly flexing. Obvious dentures revealed by his smile. Not exactly the type one would expect to be having a passionate love affair with a sexy young woman like Martha Best for several years!

"Mrs. Thompson?" Quist asked.

"Lovely lady," Betsy said, with real enthusiasm. "She's on the education committee at the plant, making sure workers' children are getting everything they're entitled to. Edna Thompson is a very special lady, sympathetic, always ready to listen. She and Mr. Thompson never had any children, but they seem to be enough for each other. Married when they were both in high school, I'm told. Almost every day Mr. Thompson has some little joke-present for her."

It didn't sound like the portrait of a wife-cheater, Quist thought.

"I'm sure Mr. Thompson could get you squared away with Captain Seaton if you asked him," Betsy said.

Quist changed the subject slightly. "People must have spent a lot of time in the last six months speculating about Martha Best," he said. "Any solid guesses about her?"

Betsy frowned. "Until now, after Sue Wilson's murder and the bombing this morning, Martha's been the main topic of conversation."

"Guesses about her love life?"

"Of course—since whatever it was, she kept it well hidden."

"Your own guess?"

"I don't really have one, Mr. Quist. I didn't come to Bridgetown till I was transferred from the Chicago office to take Martha's job—after she'd been murdered. I had nothing to go on but gossip. I never knew Martha when she was alive."

"But you listened to the talk. Who were the prime candidates?"

Betsy shrugged. "All of the big shots except my boss, Mr. Foreman. He isn't married, no reason he should have been so secretive about it. You see, Martha appeared to be completely out of circulation for about three years. Mr. Sloan, Greg Martin, Mr. Thompson, Mr. Devens—all married, happily married. But people would love to think that one of the big bosses was out of line. I suppose Mr. Martin got the most votes because he was the youngest. But Nancy Martin, his wife, is the granddaughter of Herbert Manchester, who founded the business. She's one of the major stockholders, queen of the company's social activities around the world. It would have been too dangerous for Martin to be playing games, too much in Nancy's basket he couldn't afford to lose."

"Which brings us up empty," Quist said.

"Somebody from out of town who none of us knew," Betsy suggested. "There's a whole universe out there, Mr. Quist. Cities between here and New York within driving distance—Kingston, Newburgh, Poughkeepsie, all of Westchester, all of

New York itself. Millions to choose from. Martha wanted to keep it a secret, and she managed to."

But she'd intended to reveal some secrets, Quist thought. She'd told Wally that that was what she was up to, and that what she had would damage Manchester Arms. Maybe it was a waste of time to try to guess who Martha's lover had been, except that she would have shared her "secrets" with him, whoever he was.

"I've got an errand to do, Mr. Quist," Betsy said. "If you'd like me to arrange for you to talk to Mr. Thompson about softening up Captain Seaton—?"

"Thanks, Betsy, but I've got to stay where I can be reached, in case there's some news about Lydia. I'll be at Bridgetown House in case anyone asks you."

Wait and wait and wait for a dreaded threat, or for Gardella to put the finger on Lydia's abductor. There was a message for him to call his office when he got back to the hotel. He used a pay phone in the lobby, reversing the charges. He didn't want to risk the phone in his room in case someone on the switchboard was monitoring the call. Connie Parmalee, his secretary, answered.

"Just a message from Dan," she said. "He thought you'd feel better if you knew he was on his way back. He left New York about half an hour or so ago."

"With or without Gardella?" Quist asked.

"With. I don't know what the deal was, Julian, but there was evidently no problem. Dan will call you at your hotel when he gets to Bridgetown, tell you where to meet him. He doesn't want to parade Gardella in front of watching eyes."

"Thanks for telling me, Connie."

"I wish there was more I could do," Connie said. "Nothing about Lydia?"

"No, and just pray there won't be before Gardella has a chance to look around."

Quist kept telling himself that there was no way Lydia's kidnapper could know that there was a witness to the abduction. If he didn't know, he couldn't order Gardella off.

Quist imagined he could hear the seconds ticking away at an intolerably slow pace. Sixty seconds to the minute, thirty-six hundred seconds to the hour. It would be about seven thousand more heartbeats before he could expect Dan to show up in Bridgetown with Gardella.

Quist didn't want to wait in his room. A phone call could come to him there from Seaton, or whoever had Lydia, and he would have to follow instructions. If he couldn't be reached, he couldn't be threatened. If the kidnapper couldn't contact him, that might guarantee Lydia more time.

Directly across the street from Bridgetown House was a public library. Quist crossed the street and went in. He explained that he was a stranger in town and had some time to kill. He understood that there was a newly discovered novel by Ernest Hemingway.

"If I could just sit there by the front window and browse through it," he said. "I don't want to take it out—"

He was welcomed politely. "I doubt if you can read a novel in an hour and a half, though," the librarian said. "We close at five-thirty."

Unless Garvey was delayed for some reason, that would be time enough. The seat by the window gave him a view of both the front and side entrances to Bridgetown House. He sat there watching, waiting. The whole maneuver would be absurd if Seaton were having him covered. Mr. Hemingway would have to wait for another time for his novel to be properly appreciated.

Four o'clock, four-thirty, ten minutes to five—and there was Dan's car pulling up at the side entrance. Quist dropped the book and left the library on the run. Dan had a passenger: a dark-haired, wiry little man who looked around curiously as Dan turned over his car keys to an attendant who would garage it. Quist reached them before they started into the hotel.

Tony Gardella had very bright black eyes and a broad, white smile. Quist thanked him for coming.

"Glad to do it," Gardella said. "Miss Morton is a very nice lady, been a good customer for quite a while."

"You'd know this man if you saw him again?" Quist asked. "The man she went off with?"

"Absolutely," Gardella said.

"Let's just walk down the block and I'll tell you what's cooking," Quist said. Dan didn't know about the Seaton lead, which had originated with Liz Davis after he'd headed for New York to find Gardella.

"A cop?" Gardella asked, as if he didn't like the sound of it.

"A killer-cop if he's our man," Quist said.

"So, where can I get a look at him?" Gardella asked.

"Two places we can cover," Quist said. "He could be writing up his day's report at policc headquarters. After that he could be heading for home at some point."

"So you ask for him at police headquarters and I take a look at him," Gardella said.

"If he's our man, and we ask for him, we won't see him," Quist said.

Police headquarters was just a couple of blocks away down the hill, an old stone building that had once been some kind of armory. Quist, Dan, and Gardella took a position across the street, watching the comings and goings of cops in uniform, cops in plain clothes, clerical help. There was no way to guess when Seaton would come or go.

Once again there was the painfully slow passing of time, waiting, doing nothing, hoping.

"I could call headquarters on the phone," Dan suggested. "Ask for Seaton."

"Put him on the alert," Quist said.

"Look, Julian, I'm not a dummy," Garvey said. "He'll never know who called, but we may know that he's there, in the headquarters, and we wouldn't just stand around here wasting time for him to show here when he's actually someplace else."

"I guess it's worth a try," Quist said.

Garvey headed down the block, looking for a pay phone. There had been plenty of time during the drive up from New York for Garvey to have given Gardella chapter and verse on the situation in Bridgetown.

"I'd like to nail this son of a bitch," Gardella said, his bright eyes focused on the entrance to police headquarters. "A man like that kills once, it gets easier the next time, and even easier the next time around. No problem for him to knock off Miss Morton. No conscience, no human feelings, just a wild animal."

Quist's hand closed down on Gardella's arm. "There he is!"

Captain Seaton, wearing civilian clothes, was coming out of the building, chatting with a uniformed cop.

Gardella's eyes narrowed. "Which one?"

"The one in street clothes," Quist said.

Gardella shook his head, slowly. "Not him," he said.

"Be sure, man!"

"I'm sure, Mr. Quist," Gardella said. "I never saw that man before in my life. It's not him."

It was like a balloon being deflated, Quist thought. He had been so sure that Gardella would settle things by naming Seaton. Garvey came trotting back toward them with the word that someone inside police headquarters had told him Captain Seaton had just left the office. One look at Quist and he realized that something had gone wrong.

"Seaton is not the man," Quist said.

"You're sure?" Garvey asked Gardella.

"Positive. This man here is bigger, heavier. Face not even close."

The three men stood there, staring at the building, as if they were waiting for some kind of miracle to happen.

"I've been meaning to ask you, Tony," Garvey said. "Did Sergeant Carter in New York get you together with one of those police artists who try to come up with some kind of a portrait from a description?"

Gardella nodded. "Spent what seemed like hours at it. Shape of the chin, the mouth, the eyes—over and over till it came out looking something like the guy I saw with Miss Morton. But probably his own mother wouldn't recognize him from the drawing."

"Anything special, different about the man?" Garvey asked.

Gardella shrugged. "It's summer. He was wearing some kind of linen suit. He was wearing a hat, so I couldn't see the color of his hair, but I'd guess he was blond, fair at any rate. Not as big as your Captain Seaton, like I said, but he moved like a guy in pretty good physical shape."

"Age?"

"Not a kid, not an old man," Gardella said. "So where do we look next?"

"Going to be dark in another forty-five minutes, an hour," Garvey said. "Hard to spot someone in a big city under street lights. If it isn't Seaton, we haven't a clue as to where he might hang out, where he might live. I've got just one suggestion, Julian."

"Which is?"

"Your Miss Davis. She had to be close to something, or why try to bomb her out? She thought it was Seaton. It isn't. Maybe she can come up with a second guess when she knows that. You must be pretty pooped, Julian. You want to go up to your room, get some rest, I'll go talk to her."

Quist shook his head. "I don't want to go anywhere near my room or the hotel where someone can reach me on the phone. That could be the call, with Lydia put on, then I'm given my orders."

"But wouldn't it help to hear her voice?"

"It would mean they've used her and are done with her," Quist said, his voice harsh. "I intend to stall that as long as I can."

"Well, then, let's go talk to Liz Davis. She needs warning, Julian, and knowing it isn't Seaton, she might lead us in another sensible direction."

"I've got a home phone number for her," Quist said. "Let's see if she's gone home yet."

Luck was with them this time. Liz Davis had just returned to her apartment.

"I've gotten a little paranoid about telephones in this town," Quist told her. "We've come up with something important, but I'd rather tell you in person than on the phone. I'd like to come over with Dan Garvey and a friend of ours."

"So, come!"

Liz lived in a very plush apartment building at the upper level of the city. A doorman refused them admittance until he got clearance from Miss Davis. She was, obviously, already protecting herself.

In an attractive and expensively decorated living room, Liz greeted them and was introduced to Gardella. Liz already knew why he was here.

"He's had a look at Captain Seaton," Quist told her. "He's not the man who abducted Lydia."

"Certain?" Liz asked.

"Quite certain, ma'am," Gardella said.

"But that doesn't mean you aren't close to something, Liz, else why try to bomb you out?" Quist said.

The lady sat very still on the corner of her couch, the three men grouped in front of her. "Where are my manners?" she said. "Would you fellows like a drink?"

"I think we'd all better stay cold sober until we get on the right road and come to the end of it," Quist said. "What could you have been looking for, Liz, that got them scared of you?"

"You mean before today and yesterday, which means before Sue Wilson and before Eddie Lukins in my car?"

Quist nodded. "It was Martha Best's boyfriend, probably her killer, you've been looking for for months. Have you come close to something you haven't told me about?"

"No, and I was probably wasting my time."

"Not if someone decided you'd better be stopped," Garvey said.

"Maybe it's silly," Liz said, "but I started thinking about the mechanics of a long-term love affair that has to be kept hidden. It's not like a one-night stand. You have to have a regular place to go."

"That shouldn't be hard in a city of this size," Garvey said. "Dozens of quiet little apartments that could be rented."

"It's not quite as easy as that," Liz said. "The men I thought might have been involved with Martha—men at Manchester

Arms, like Mark Foreman, Seymour Sloan, Greg Martin, Jay Thompson, Ted Devens—are as well known in this city as famous movie stars. They couldn't go somewhere day after day, week after week, month after month with a lady they shouldn't be with without being seen and the word getting around."

"Another city, another town," Garvey suggested.

"Except for Mark Foreman, who didn't have to hide anything," Liz said, "these men all had social obligations they couldn't duck. Martha had a very rigid business schedule. She and her lover had to have a place to which they could escape for an hour or two and then get back to their regular schedules. There couldn't be time for travel to some other place."

"And you got some place?" Quist asked.

"I am, was, on the way," Liz said. "Manchester Arms owns a lot of real estate in this city. It's a good investment. The individual men own property in addition to their own homes. I checked out the tax records to find out who owned what."

"And . . . ?"

"The men, themselves, own nothing that wasn't occupied by a tenant of some sort, families. Manchester Arms owns some old buildings near the factory that are out of use, deserted. Could Martha and her man set up an apartment for themselves in one of those old buildings? Just step out of the factory, get lost for a couple of hours. If they were seen leaving, it would just look as though they'd been working late. Manchester Arms goes around the clock, day and night shifts. Someone who belonged there, even coming or going at the oddest hours, wouldn't attract any particular attention. Be the perfect kind of setup for a man who had to hide his goings-on."

"You talk to someone about this?" Quist asked.

Liz shook her head. "No—or yes and no. I may have speculated to some friends about the mechanics of keeping a love affair secret. Everybody had a guess. I could write a book on how a man can cheat on his wife. But when I got thinking about properties owned by Manchester Arms and its big-shot people, I stopped talking about it. I didn't want there to be any chance that what I was looking into would get back to anyone at Manchester."

"The town clerk?" Garvey suggested. "You say you were looking at tax records."

"They aren't secret," Liz said. "I didn't have to explain why I wanted to look at them. Plus I'm a reporter, and the clerk knows that. Looking into records of one sort or another is not too unusual for me."

"So you didn't tip your mitt," Garvey said.

"Not to the clerk. But later—perhaps—"

"What?"

"There's one old building, actually attached to the Manchester plant, that used to be a machine shop. Some time ago—several years, I think, when they retooled or something—the building went out of regular use. They store things on the main floor—office supplies, odds and ends. I think the upper floors aren't used. I went there one afternoon just to look around and got unlucky. I ran into Bart Havens, Manchester's security chief. He, laughingly, warned me off. Outsiders weren't allowed to be wandering around inside Manchester's property."

"The Telly Savalas character?" Garvey asked.

"Yes. I had to take off, but I planned to come back later sometime. I never did because things began to happen. You and Wally came to town, Julian, and the election campaign got top priority in my world. Then Sue Wilson. Now this."

"Excuse me, please," Gardella said. "You talking about someone who looks like Telly Savalas?"

"Yeah," Garvey said. "He's head of security at Manchester."

Gardella's bright red tongue ran along his lower lip. "When Sergeant Carter in New York was trying to get me to describe the man who took off with Miss Morton to the police artist, he asked me if he looked anything like some movie actor—that would be a starting point for the artist. I told him Telly Savalas!"

"Oh, brother!" Garvey said.

Havens, Lydia's kidnapper? Quist tried to remember what Havens's alibi had been for that Wednesday morning. He'd been wandering around town talking to contacts of his about Sue Wilson's murder. Had anybody bothered to check that out?

"So we go to the cops and let them put the heat on Havens," Garvey said.

"No!" Quist said sharply. "No way to keep it a secret for thirty seconds if you talk to anyone about it. If Havens is holding Lydia, maybe in the very place where Martha and her boyfriend had their love nest, he could finish her off before we have a chance to turn around."

"That's it, of course," Garvey said. "He had to get rid of Liz before she went back again to check on that building. She would go back because she's a good reporter and she doesn't give up."

"Let's be dead sure," Quist said. "Let Gardella have a look at him so we know for certain."

"You know where he lives, Liz?" Garvey asked.

"No, but let's try the phone book. He must be listed. People have to be able to reach him."

It was there, an apartment building not far from Manchester.

"We'll go call him, and if he's not there, we'll go and wait for him to show," Garvey said.

"I still don't quite understand why you don't go to the police," Liz Davis said.

"The only thing in the world that matters to me," Quist said in a tight, cold voice, "is Lydia. She can hang Havens, if he's the man. If he's warned that we're onto him, he won't give her that chance."

Liz called Havens's number for them on her phone. There was no answer. So he wasn't home yet. It was about eight o'clock in the evening, still fairly light on the city streets. The only thing they could do was go to his apartment building and wait for him. When he showed, Quist could stop him, engage him in conversation while Gardella made certain about him.

"For God's sake, Liz, don't tell anyone that Gardella is here in town and why," Quist said as they were leaving.

"Count on me, Julian," Liz said.

The apartment house where Havens lived was only three or four blocks from Liz Davis's building. Just in the time it would take them to get there, Havens could slip in and keep them waiting forever. They decided that Garvey would stay with Liz. When Quist and Gardella got to Havens's building, they'd phone back, and Liz would try calling Havens again. If Havens didn't answer, Garvey would rejoin them. It was elaborate, but to inquire at the building for Havens might only result in his being warned.

Quist and Gardella quickly walked the few blocks to Havens's building, found a pay phone, and called Liz. They waited in the booth for her to call back. She did. No answer on Havens's phone. They had a chance to catch him when he returned. Garvey was on his way.

Daylight faded. The front entrance to Havens's building was brightly lighted, so there was no danger of missing the man when he came home. Quist and Gardella sat down on the front steps of a small house across the way to wait and watch. Garvey joined them after a few minutes.

"Son of a bitch could be with Lydia right now," Garvey said, "trying to reach you on the phone at Bridgetown House, to put her on the phone to you, Julian, and warn you off."

Time moved on with the same dreadful slowness that it had for most of the day. People came and went, in and out of the apartment building across the way, but there was no sign of Havens. The facts they had went around and around in Quist's aching head. One alibi Havens had: He'd not killed Martha Best. He'd been out of the country the night of the blizzard. The man who had killed her had acquired Havens as an accomplice when he returned. That man had to know about

Lydia, where she was being held. If they mishandled Havens, that second man would still be free to dispose of Lydia.

An hour went by, two hours. Traffic thinned out, and the stream of people returning home to the apartment building had thinned to a trickle.

"Hey, you guys! Park your butts somewhere else. This is my house." A big black-haired man who looked ready to take on the world was glowering down at them.

"Sorry," Quist said. "We were waiting for a friend to turn up across the way."

"Well, wait somewhere else."

At that precise moment, Bart Havens turned the corner at the end of the block and headed toward the apartment house. Quist pointed him out to Gardella.

"That's him," Gardella said. "Same tan-colored linen suit, same straw hat. No question."

They crossed the street and were there when Havens started for the door. He recovered quickly from his surprise, and that white-toothed professional smile moved across his lips.

"Well, well, well," he said. "A reception committee." He glanced at Gardella. "I don't think I've had the pleasure."

"Tony Gardella is a friend of Dan's and mine from New York," Quist said. "We were waiting for you. We have some questions you could help us with."

"So, come on in," Havens said. "I can't give you too much time. I keep early hours and need to get some sleep."

They went into the apartment building and boarded a self-service elevator. Havens pressed the button for the seventh floor. He lived pretty well for a company cop, Quist thought. At the seventh floor Havens took a thick bunch of keys from his trouser pocket and opened the first door to the right of the elevator, switched on some lights, and waved his callers in.

"I can give you just about enough time to drink one beer," Havens said.

"It won't take that long if you give us the answer we want," Garvey said. "Where is she?"

Havens's smile seemed to freeze. "Where is she? Who?"

"Lydia Morton," Garvey said.

"That's your lady, isn't it, Quist?"

"That's my lady," Quist said. "Tony Gardella saw you pick her up in New York."

"Oh, come on! That's absurd," Havens said.

"Tony has a newsstand just across from our office," Quist said. "He saw Lydia coming that morning. She gets a paper from him every day. He turned to take care of another customer, and when he looked back, he saw Lydia getting into your car with you."

"I never saw this guy before in my life!" Havens said. "I haven't been in New York in weeks. He saw wrong."

"This is the man," Gardella said, his dark eyes very bright.

"No way at all," Havens said. "I wouldn't know your Miss Morton if I saw her, and I certainly didn't see her. Was it Wednesday? I wasn't there."

"Same suit, same hat, same Telly Savalas face," Gardella said.

"I've heard that before," Havens said, "that I look like Savalas. Maybe that's who you saw, buster."

"Is she in the building next to Manchester Arms where you saw Liz Davis snooping around?" Quist asked. "Is that why you tried to kill Liz with that car bomb?"

Havens's smile was totally gone. "I've had about enough of this, you creeps!" he said. "Take off!"

"When you tell us," Garvey said.

Havens made a quick sort of half-turn and spun back with a gun he'd been carrying in a shoulder holster, and it was aimed at them. Quist and Garvey were in his direct line of fire. "Now! Go!" he said.

Tony Gardella was directly behind Havens. He moved forward, and Quist saw the blade of a pocket knife glittering in the light from the ceiling fixture. Gardella pricked the skin on the side of Havens's neck with it.

"You better drop that gun, pal, if you don't want your throat cut," Gardella said. It sounded for real.

Havens, his mouth twitching, hesitated a moment, then let the gun drop with a thud to the carpet.

"Now, let's get on with it," Garvey said. "You can tell us what we have to know, or we can kill you right here and now. You can tell us where Lydia is and she comes out of it safe and sound or else."

"Of course, when you stop playing Boy Scout heroes, I'll have you locked up for life!" Havens said.

"Your keys," Garvey said. "And don't take your time about it."

"What the hell do you want my keys for?"

"If Lydia's locked up in that Manchester building, you've probably got the key to her jail right there on your key ring. Do you want to give it to me, or do I take it?"

Havens took the heavy key ring from his pocket and held it out to Garvey. "Take it and go!" he said.

"It's not quite as simple as that, chum," Garvey said, taking the keys. "We wouldn't want you to get lonely." He handed the keys to Quist, and then bent down and picked up Havens's gun. He spun the cylinder on it. "My, my, it's loaded," he said in a sarcastic tone. "A Manchester gun, probably loaded with Manchester bullets, carried by a Manchester tough guy, with a Manchester big shot standing behind him. Quite a story for Liz Davis when we can get it to her."

"I have a permit to carry that rod," Havens said. "When three jerks try to strong-arm you in your own home, you have a right to try to protect yourself."

"A sad story," Garvey said. "Here's how the rest of it goes, if Julian agrees. Julian, you and Tony take off for that old building Liz Davis was looking at. If Lydia's there, she's locked in a room somewhere. You'll probably find the key on butcher boy's key ring. You should be the one to find Lydia. I'm staying here with Telly Savalas. If he decides to get obstreperous or call his boss to warn him, my conscience will let me blow his head off without any hesitation at all." He hefted the gun. "Nice balance. Too bad you won't be around, Havens, to write

Manchester a testimonial if I have to use it." He turned to Quist. "Call me when you do—or don't—find Lydia."

The telephone rang. Garvey hesitated, and then, with the gun aimed at Havens, picked up the phone. "Hello. Who? Havens? I think you've got the wrong number." He put the phone down. Seconds later it rang again, and this time he let it keep ringing until it cut out.

"Go, Julian," Garvey said.

Out on the street, Quist turned to Gardella. "There's no reason for you to get involved in this, Tony," he said. "It could be dangerous."

"I think of Miss Morton as a friend," Gardella said. "I'd like to go with you. I'd like to help."

"You already saved that last ball game for us," Quist said. "I owe you."

"I'd still like to go with you," Gardella said.

It was after eleven, but the Manchester plant was lighted from top to bottom, the night shift in full swing. There would be, Quist guessed, people coming and going. They couldn't let themselves be seen nosing around. From across the way they could see the building Liz Davis had mentioned, a semi-abandoned warehouse. There were no lights at all there; it was a dark hulk rising up into the night sky.

"Probably locked up," Gardella said.

"And if we're right about Havens, I probably have the key," Quist said.

With no one in sight, Quist and Gardella darted across the street into the shadows of the warehouse. Quist tried a door opening onto the alley between the factory and the old building. It wasn't locked. They went in. Inside there was just enough light from the factory windows for them to see stacks of boxes and crates—office supplies, as Liz Davis had suggested. Somewhere on the upper floors? Somewhere up above, a locked door with Lydia behind it?

Quist and Gardella climbed a dark stairway to the second floor. Four doors opened off a wide hall. None of them was locked. There wasn't anything in any of the four rooms, no furnishings, no boxes or machinery stored. The third floor, geographically a duplicate of the second, produced the same result. No locked doors, nothing stored in the rooms. The fourth floor was the top—the end of the line. Quist's hopes were dwindling.

The first door on the fourth floor was unlocked like all the others, the room beyond it bare. The second door was also not locked, but inside was a difference. In the dim light they could see the frame and mattress of a double bed, a bureau, a couple of wooden armchairs. They were all pushed to one side.

Quist stood very still, his heart starting to pound.

"You smell anything, Tony?" he asked Gardella.

He sniffed and shook his head. "What should I be smelling?"

Quist would have known it anywhere, the faint scent of Lydia's perfume. He saw a little spot of white on the floor just beyond the bed and went to it. A handkerchief! It was Lydia's handkerchief, her initials embroidered in one corner. Quist had given that handkerchief, along with others like it, to Lydia last Christmas. He held the handkerchief up to his nose.

"She was here!" he said, his voice unsteady.

Gardella went quickly down the hall and checked the last two rooms. They were unlocked, nothing inside.

"They've taken her somewhere else," Quist said when Gardella reported. "But where? In the whole goddamned world, where?"

This room, Quist told himself, was what was left of what had once been a love nest for Martha Best and her boyfriend, a place only they knew about until that relationship had ended in murder. Then the murderer needed help in covering his tracks and hired Havens to help him dispose of Martha's body, and eventually to trick Lydia into coming with him to Bridgetown and to this room, which had been her jail. Until how long ago?

A pay phone wasn't easy to find at that time of night, the few bars and restaurants near the factory having closed early.

But there was a street-corner booth about a block from the Manchester factory. Quist called Havens's apartment and heard Garvey's voice on the phone. In a shaken voice he reported what they'd found.

"She was there, but she's gone, Dan. Dear God, it may be too late now."

"Get back here," Garvey said. "Maybe I can soften this bum up a little while you're on the way. There has to be a way to move, and move fast."

"I wish I could believe that," Quist said.

Bart Havens, the Telly Savalas lookalike, had lost all his bravado when Quist and Gardella got back to the apartment. He sat in an armchair, gripping the arms with hands whose knuckles were white from pressure.

"I've been spelling it out for our friend here," Garvey said. "He won't name the man who hired him, but that man will name him when the time comes. I've also made it clear to him that his trial, sentence, and execution may take place right here in this room if he doesn't open up. I think he's starting to believe me."

Quist knew they would never kill this man. Only someone like Havens himself, who was capable of that kind of violence, might believe it. The other man, Havens's employer, almost certainly had Lydia now, if she was still alive. Now there was no place to look except in a void.

"The first thing," Garvey said, "is to find out where these characters are—Foreman and his top shots."

"Home in bed," Havens muttered.

"Let's call them on the phone, tell them there's some kind of crisis at the plant and they're needed," Dan said. "Then when they're all there, face them with what you have."

It was as good as anything Quist could think of. He began making the calls, first to Seymour Sloan. The man himself answered.

"Mr. Sloan? I've been told to call you. There's some kind of crisis at the plant. You're needed there."

"What kind of crisis?"

"I'm sorry, sir. I was just told to call you."

"Who is this?"

Quist put down the receiver. The calls to Thompson and Devens were almost duplicates of the one to Sloan.

"They'll call back the plant and find there isn't any crisis," Havens said.

"A phony call is a crisis in itself," Garvey said. "They'll turn up to find out what's cooking."

The call to Greg Martin's house was a little different. A crisp female voice answered.

"Mrs. Martin?"

"Yes, this is Nancy Martin."

"I need to talk to your husband, Mrs. Martin."

"Do you have any idea what time of night it is?" The woman sounded angry. Quist remembered the handsome red-haired woman who had been the "doorwoman" at the Women's Rights meeting. A red-haired temper, he thought.

"There's some kind of crisis at the plant, Mrs. Martin. He's needed there."

"If you were doing your job, man, you'd know that that's where he is, at the plant. He's been there all night as far as I know." The woman banged down the receiver.

"So, go talk to them," Garvey said.

"Before you go, Quist, let me say it one more time," Bart Havens said. "I didn't murder Martha Best. I wasn't in the United States that night. You know it and the cops know it. I didn't kill Sue Wilson in your hotel room. I'm a professional. I don't get caught with my pants down! I didn't set a bomb in Liz Davis's car, and you don't have a shred of evidence to prove otherwise."

"But you did go to New York on Wednesday, persuade Miss Morton to come back here with you, and imprison her in the old warehouse. We have an eyewitness to that," Garvey said.

"Get going, Julian. There may still be time. I'll stay with our friend here and listen to whatever other lies he may have to tell. If you think it will help to produce him down at the plant, I'll drag him there."

"We didn't call Foreman," Quist said.

"He'll be there," Garvey said. "Someone has already notified him of some kind of trouble. Take Tony with you. His evidence is what they'll need."

The plant didn't look any different from the way it had a few hours before, but a uniformed night watchman barred their entrance at the front door.

"I want to see Mr. Foreman," Quist said.

"No visitors at this time of night," the watchman said. "What makes you think Mr. Foreman would be here this late?"

"I know he is," Quist said. "Just call him and tell him it's Julian Quist, that I'm here with an important witness. Tell him that I'm the one who made the phone calls. He'll understand."

The watchman went off and came back in a moment, grinning. "The boss says I'm to bring you up to him on the double."

Foreman, Thompson, Devens, and Sloan were all in the president's office, all angry.

"What the hell kind of game are you playing, Quist?" Foreman demanded.

"Where's Greg Martin?" Quist asked.

"Probably got sensible and turned over and went back to sleep," Seymour Sloan said.

"His wife told me he'd been at the plant most of the night," Quist said.

"Well, she was mistaken," Foreman said. "I'll be damned if I'm going to put up with this kind of hocus-pocus, Quist."

"Let me spread it out for you," Quist said. He explained who Tony Gardella was, how he'd witnessed Lydia's being driven away from outside her office on Wednesday morning, how Gardella had come to Bridgetown to see if he could identify the kidnapper.

"And could he?" Foreman asked.

"Bart Havens," Quist said. "Beyond a doubt."

"Havens?" Foreman almost laughed. "Why would Havens be interested in your Miss Morton?"

"The price was right," Quist said, his voice grim. "The price was right to persuade him to help get Martha Best's body back into her car after she'd been murdered. The price was right to search my room and Wally Best's, looking for something Martha may have given her brother that would point to the murderer. That job was botched, and Sue Wilson had to die. She knew the man she found in my room. She would have known all of you by sight, Bart Havens included. The price was right to involve him in the attempt to dispose of Liz Davis by putting a bomb in her car. She'd discovered, though she didn't know it, the place where Martha Best had carried on with one of you for a couple of years. Havens saw her nosing around that warehouse. She had to be silenced before she realized how close she was to blowing the whole situation wide open."

"Farfetched!" Seymour Sloan said.

"Havens and any one of you had access to the kind of explosive that was used to blow up the car. You make that kind of stuff right here in this factory."

"Just a minute," Foreman said. "Why hasn't your Miss Morton been used to scare you off, Quist?"

"They'd have to put her on the phone to me, live, if they hoped to scare me off," Quist said. "I have been, quite deliberately, not reachable by phone for a long time. I don't trust your hotel. I haven't answered the phone in my room since Sue Wilson died there. But now, since we've got Havens, one of you knows that the ball game is nearly over. One of you has moved Lydia. Is it just to hide her again, or is it to dispose of her? She can name whichever one of you it is who's behind all this along with Havens."

"You've been to the police with all of this?" Foreman asked.

"No, because at first we were sure Captain Seaton was the man who was being paid to help one of you. Gardella turned us on to Havens. We've got him where he can't make a move or warn his partner, but whichever one of you it is somehow knew and took Lydia from where she was being held in the warehouse."

"I still say it's farfetched," Sloan said.

"I promise you," Quist said, and his voice was unsteady with anger, "if Lydia isn't returned to me, alive and unharmed, in a very short time, I will finish you off, one by one. You think that's farfetched, Sloan? Quite simply, I have no reason to want to go on living if Lydia is gone."

Foreman seemed to take charge. It was his custom to take charge. "All right, friends, we all know that none of us here is involved in this horror story," he said. "But the lady is missing. She was held in our warehouse. She has been taken somewhere else. Each one of you has a department here in the plant. Go to your own area and have it searched inch by inch. I think I understand what Quist is feeling. If I were in his shoes I'd probably make the same kind of wild threats he's making. Let's find Miss Morton."

Sloan, Thompson, and Devens all took off without a word. Quist, left alone with Foreman, had the feeling they'd all been given the chance to escape. He'd had no way to stop them.

"You got a gun?" Foreman asked.

Quist didn't answer.

"I'm not trying to find out how safe I am," Foreman said with a tight-lipped smile. "I want to be sure you're safe." He opened the top drawer of his desk and produced two handguns. He handed one of them to Quist. "Check it out. It's loaded. Be sure you know how to handle the safety catch on it."

"I'm familiar with this," Quist said, hefting the gun. "What do you expect me to do with it?"

"Let's not pretend," Foreman said. "The man we're after is Greg Martin. I know these men all too well. Greg's the only one capable of what you suggest. And he has a boat down at the yacht club. He often goes down there when he wants to be alone to think and work, or whatever other things he may want to do in private."

"You think he may have taken Lydia there?"

"Your guess is as good as mine," Foreman said. "Let's go."

It wasn't more than a couple of hundred yards from the Manchester plant to the river's edge and a small yacht club where several boats were moored. Foreman pointed out a handsome motor launch tied to the dock.

"Greg's," he said. "You stay undercover. I'll go aboard. I've often come here to talk to him. If he's there, I'll maneuver him to the far side of the boat to 'talk.' You come aboard and look for your lady."

Foreman made no effort to conceal his approach, pale moonlight making him plainly visible. He'd just reached the little gangway that led from the dock to the boat when Martin appeared.

"Oh, it's you, Mark," Quist heard him say.

The rest of the conversation was too quiet for Quist to hear, but Foreman and Martin walked slowly around the stern of the ship to the other side of the cabin structure, out of Quist's view. Quist moved quickly down the dock and down the gangway onto the boat, opened the cabin door, and went in. In the semi-darkness there was nothing to see but simple furnishings. At the far end of the cabin was another door, probably leading to sleeping quarters, Quist thought.

Quist opened that door and stood for a moment, heart pounding against his ribs. Lydia was here. Lydia, with a wide strip of plastic tape across her mouth, her hands behind the back of the chair in which she was sitting, probably tied there. Her eyes were as wide as saucers.

Quist made a quick gesture for silence, went to her, and peeled the tape off her mouth as gently as he could. "Darling, darling, darling," he was whispering.

"Oh, Julian!"

He went around the chair and saw that Lydia's wrists were held together by handcuffs.

"I just may have the key to these," he said. He took Havens's keys out of his pocket, found what he was looking for, unlocked the cuffs, and set Lydia free.

She was in his arms, crying softly.

"It's not quite over, love," Quist said, holding her very close.

They walked out through the cabin and onto the deck of the launch. Quist had one arm around Lydia and in his other hand held the gun Foreman had given him. They walked around to the offshore side of the boat where Foreman and Martin were leaning on the rail, looking out at the river.

"Success!" Quist said, in a loud clear voice.

Both men spun around. Martin made a kind of animal sound of despair and fumbled at his pocket.

"Forget it, Greg!" Foreman said. "This is pointed right at your heart!" Holding his gun at Martin's chest, Foreman reached into the man's pocket and relieved him of his gun. "Lady okay?" Foreman asked.

"Breathing, walking," Quist said. " 'Okay' covers a lot of territory. This is the man who brought you here, Lyd?"

"Here to the boat," Lydia said. "Another man brought me up from New York, held me in a building up here."

"We've got him, too," Quist said.

Just how the next hour or so took place Quist couldn't have told anyone later. The police came, and Martin was arrested. Havens was arrested in his own apartment. Lydia was taken to Maggie Nolan's house at the top of the hill, where she would be safe and with friends. Quist, Garvey, and Mark Foreman went to police headquarters to file formal charges against Martin and Havens.

Quist's main concern was to get back to Lydia, but as he listened to the story Martin told the district attorney, he found himself having an extraordinary reaction. He actually felt sympathy for a man who had murdered two women and planned the murder of a third, a plan that had backfired and taken the life of an innocent boy.

Martin began with a description of his marriage to Nancy Manchester, granddaughter of the founder of Manchester Arms.

" 'The little princess,' the old man called her. And Nancy plays the role of princess. She has to control everything and every person she touches. My career, when we married, was on Success Street, but—if you can understand—I had to walk the dog whenever she told me to. Our romance died before it began. I was just her slave. And then, one day, Martha Best came into my life. Long and short, we started to have a passionate kind of thing together. We had to be very careful. I set up a room in the old warehouse where we could meet. Coming and going from the plant was routine for us. Nobody noticed. And so, almost every day for two years, we were happily together. Then—then it was proposed that I should run for mayor. That was bad—for Martha and me; the press would be following me everywhere. While the campaign was going on, after I was in the mayor's office—I was bound to win—Martha and I would have to be apart. I couldn't return to her. It would finish me at Manchester. The night I told Martha was the night of the blizzard. She had parked down the street, expecting to stay a few moments. But when I told her that our affair was over, she blew her stack, started to scream and yell at me. I tried to quiet her because people on the night shift might hear, but it got louder and louder. Finally I—I took her by the neck to try to choke off her yelling. And when she was silent, I let go. She slipped down to the floor and—and she was dead. God help me, I'd killed her. No intention to do any such thing, of course, but there it was."

A kind of hysterical panic took him over, Martin told them. He'd left her there and gone home, trying to figure out what to do. It could be the end of his world, the end of his life. He'd finally decided that he would have to cover it up if he were to survive. But he would need help. He couldn't make a move himself without the risk of being caught red-handed. He thought of Bart Havens, a man who spent most of his life in a climate of terrorism. Bart, properly paid, could get him out of this.

"He had a price," Martin said, "and he took it on as though it was a game that pleased him. It was he who moved Martha's body from the warehouse into the trunk of her own car. Then Wally Best appeared on the scene to run against me. I—I had written a score of love letters to Martha over the years. Had she given them to Wally? Would he and Quist use them against me? Havens suggested that their rooms at Bridgetown House be searched. He was like a Svengali to me, told me what to do to save myself, and I did it. Havens loaned me one of his own passkeys. I searched Wally's room. Nothing. I went to Quist's room and started searching there when the Wilson girl walked in—day maid's duties. She knew who I was, of course. I struck her with a vase that was there on the table. I kept striking her with it until she was dead." Martin shuddered. "I—I had nothing against her. I loved Martha. It—it just happened that way."

Martin took a deep breath. "Then Liz Davis had been sneaking around the warehouse. Havens caught her, warned her off, but he was convinced she was on the trail. We had to silence her. I was in a bloody fog by then, a kind of trance. Havens knew best, knew what we had to do. He—he stole a bomb out of supplies here, but I had to connect it to the car. I'm an electrical engineer, you know, designed some of those bombs for army use. I attached the bomb so that it would go off when Liz Davis stepped on the gas. Only it was that unfortunate kid who tried to move the car for her."

Then, after a long silence: "Then tonight I—I went to see Havens at his apartment. What next? Quist and Garvey were there with him, and as I stood outside the apartment door, I heard them talking about the warehouse. Havens had decided to lure Miss Morton up here to use against Quist in case he got too close. Well, he was too close now. Soon he'd go to the warehouse, and the ball game would be over. So I went down to the warehouse, brought the girl down to the boat, and made her my prisoner there."

"You didn't kill her," Quist said in a hollow voice. "Why not?"

"I'd reached a point where I had to wait for Havens to tell me what to do," Martin said. Havens's sick, terrorist mentality had changed Martin, once a relatively normal man, into a monster.

There were dozens of questions, none of which Quist really heard. Martin and Havens were, together, responsible for three murders with no possible way out for either of them.

It was daylight when Quist left the men and then a tearful Wally and got back up the hill to Maggie Nolan's place. The old woman met him at the front door. "Brave girl, that Lydia of yours. Dr. Tobin's been here to check on her, and there's nothing physically wrong with her. Psychologically, she's suffered a bad shock. What she needs mainly is you, Julian."

"That's all I need, too," Quist said. "Just Lydia. Where is she?"